Dawn!

My Triumph over Abuse and Trauma

DR. SHARON JOSHUA JOHN

When love beckons to you, follow him,

Though his ways are hard and steep.

And when his wings enfold you, yield to him,

Though the sword hidden among his pinions may wound you.

And when he speaks to you, believe in him,

Though his voice may shatter your dreams

As the north wind lays waste the garden.

For even as love crowns you so shall he crucify you.

Even as he is for your growth so is he for your pruning.

Khalil Gibran

This book holds a special place in my heart and is dedicated to the cherished memory of my late husband, Andy. He was the one who brought the profound joys of being a wife and a mother into my life, giving me our beloved children. Their love, encouragement, and unwavering support have been the backbone of this endeavor.

I owe a deep gratitude to my late grandmother Nainamma, my father's mother, whose love knew no bounds. She gave me my name and cherished me as her eldest grandchild, leaving an indelible mark on my heart.

My beloved parents deserve a world of thanks. They instilled in me the powerful virtues of love and forgiveness, teaching me to find the silver lining, no matter the storms life may bring. Their lessons on embracing life's beauty amidst turmoil have been a guiding light, encouraging me to hold onto hope and cherish every moment.

Very importantly, my children for being supportive and encouraging me to write. They had been unaware of the traumatic incidents that took place in my past and seemed astonished upon learning about several of the events, while I was writing this book. Their childhood, filled with trauma in the absence of a father, was not a normal one. I have instilled faith in God, compassion, and kindness in them. I believe these are the essential qualities for every human being. I consider myself privileged that God has chosen me to be the mother of my children. I trust I have been a good guardian since He placed them under my care. After all, He is the giver of life.

Preface

I have chosen to share my life as an ambitious, passionately successful global corporate leader and not as a victim of domestic violence. I am an immigrant from India who came to the United States more than twenty years ago. I consider myself a conqueror and an 'overcomer.' I have written this book for the many women who suffer in silence, hoping that reading about my life will help them somehow. This is my journey and my story. I choose to own everything that makes me human. While writing this book, hurtful memories assailed me, and I suffered many moments of emotional torment. As always, I paused, smiled, and said to myself, I have made it so far through this maze of life, with all its twists, turns, and blind alleys, and continue to do so, injured, healing, and unbroken. I take each day with happiness and gratitude, knowing I am in a much better place today than I was years ago.

Writing this book has been a cathartic experience. Domestic violence overturned my life and my perspective. I had no idea that my life would be filled with so many challenges that would prompt the writing of this book. The world has always judged me; some people are hateful and despise me, some love me, some applaud me. Often, many do not understand me. And yet, at the end of it all, I realize I stand tall and unapologetic.

It took me several years and several losses to pen the story of my survival and the fulfillment of my dreams, which still hold me in awe. Time has helped me crystallize my thinking about how staying in an abusive relationship changed my entire life and perspective forever. Life was a vicious cycle for more than two decades, and I was the hamster on the wheel — always racing and running without stopping. I now realize that I am no longer bound to or by my past. My past did help me become braver and stronger. I have long removed the shackles that held me back and moved ahead with great gusto, confidence, hope, and peace.

I hope my experiences will give you a sense of why I stayed in an abusive relationship for 19 years. When I was ready to give up, 'prayer and hope' came to my rescue. I have no regrets and do not ask for sympathy. Because I would do it all over again if I had to. The past has taught me to love myself better and know that it is acceptable to invest in myself. I still struggle to do this at times, but I have learned to let go of the emotional baggage that had weighed me down for several years. This is still a process, and I am at it daily.

If you find something in my story that doesn't quite resonate with you, I hope you'll remember that we all experience and interpret life differently.

Sharing our stories openly and without fear of being judged is what truly sets us free and begins the healing process. My greatest wish is that by the end of this book, you'll feel empowered to share your own story, potentially changing a life mired in despair.

To protect privacy and honor memories, I've chosen to write under a pseudonym and alter names. I've learnt to cherish the simple joys life offers and am forever grateful for the divine grace that has shaped who I am and who I'm still becoming.

A huge thank you to everyone who helped me turn the pages of my life into this book.

A sincere thanks to Dr Vasantha Chary, whose encouragement and guidance were instrumental in the completion of my doctoral dissertation. In the six years I worked toward my Ph.D., I was able to surmount several personal and professional challenges under her guidance.

Special thanks to Ganesh Vancheeswaran for being patient, supportive, and kind while I wrote this book. In the past two years, I gave up writing for several months due to personal grief and loss. Ganesh has taken a special interest in me and has motivated and encouraged me. He is more than an editor and has become a wonderful, dear friend across the Atlantic.

Contents

Dr. Sharon Joshua John

My Childhood and Teenage

I am the Rose of Sharon and the lily of the valleys. I was named by my beloved grandmother, my dad's mom, who was a powerful influencer much before the rise of social media influencers. In my world, you can either be an influencer, gently caressing and nudging somebody with strength and leaving sweet, long-lasting memories, or you can ravage another person's life, wounding and scarring them, changing the trajectory of their life and often causing them to veer off into the darker alleys of destiny. Naimamma, as I used to call my paternal grandmother, was an influencer of the former kind, her gentle, loving kindness instilling warmth and depth in the lives of those she came to touch. Even at the age of seven, I remember that the greyest of her grey hair held a strange fascination for me. Never until then had I seen such curly grey hair! She always kept it bundled at the nape of her neck.

I have beautiful memories of my early childhood when my little family lived with my Nainamma in her home in East Maredpally, Hyderabad, India. Hyderabad is still a charming place and is called the city of pearls. It is known for its historical grandeur, incredible monuments, world-famous biryani, chai, and pearls.

I recall the sense of comfort and safety I felt late at night every time I snuggled with my Nainamma under the warm light-green blanket. I would sneak into the blanket when she had covered herself. She'd light some coal in an earthen plate and slowly add her asthma medication to the burning coal. She'd then sit hunched on her bed and breathe the fumes from this burning medication. I would huddle with her, much to the chagrin of my mother. My mother feared that I would become asthmatic, too, whereas I somehow thought it was beneficial to breathe these medicated vapors. Nainamma inhaled the vapors for a good night's rest before we tuned into the Herbert Armstrong radio show. We listened to him religiously at 9 pm every day. Though I never understood his message, I listened to the program simply because I thought it was all grown-up business to listen to the radio. For the same reason, I'd browse through her favorite magazine, *Plain Truth*. That was the first book I read besides other historical books.

Nainamma was a Telugu teacher at Keys High School, Secunderabad. Nainamma lost her husband, my grandfather, in her early forties. Widowed, she was left to fend for herself and her seven children — three girls and four boys. Though I am my own person and a child of several circumstances, I share some strange similarities with her, as my dad sometimes used to say. Both of us lost our husbands when we were young. The law of nature tells us that death parts one's spouse, but until then, it is rightly said that 'What God has joined together let no man put asunder.' The law of the Universe allows one to leave their mortal coils at a ripe old age when they have seen their grandchildren and, sometimes, even their great-grandchildren. My grandfather's death was tragic, and so was my husband, Andy's. Grandpa's first death anniversary fell on a Good Friday, as did Andy's. These similarities seem strange because my husband and grandfather were poles apart. I never saw my grandfather; he left for his heavenly abode before my birth.

After Grandpa's death, Nainamma returned to school to complete her education. She studied under the great Maria Montessori after she had seven children! Similarly, I continued my education amidst great difficulties when my first child was merely a few months old. Nainamma ensured that I would never forget that age is not an obstacle to completing education and that education is wealth that no one can ever take away. She always said, 'Education from the womb to the tomb.' I have held on to this belief, and my education has indeed brought me a long way — all the way from Hyderabad, India, to America. I tell my kids, even to this day, that there is no 'right age' to get an education and that it can be done at any time; no task must be left unfinished as long as you possess the breath of life. In moments of despair, I counsel myself that there is 'hope beyond hope' and that I can do it. I can make a change; I am not dead yet; I still have the breath of life.

Looking back, I understand more clearly why the morbidity of death does not disturb me easily. I am often fascinated, even to this day, when I see a body devoid of life. It's strange how one addresses this human form without the breath of life as a 'body.' No one refers to the dead person by their name anymore. It is as if the person's entire personality ceases to exist when their soul departs from their body. Nobody calls their loved ones by their name. Instead, they say, 'Don't touch the body,' 'Let's move the body,' and 'Let's view the body.' Strange!

I was barely ten years old when, in my little mind, I decided that death was a good thing. It is the end of suffering, and happy are those who are gone, though it causes great grief and pain for the ones left behind. Healing comes, and they say the wounds heal, but the scars remain. I think I wear my scars quite well. Though the wounds sometimes hurt, you somehow learn to live with them.

After all, the life we have today must have some meaning to others; one has to live for the benefit of others. In the end, what do we carry, nothing! All these years, I have never heard anyone except my grandmother pray this way. These used to be her exact words: 'God, bring me into your kingdom since my work on earth is done. I am prepared, Take me.' Every day, she prayed for everyone else and, lastly, for herself. She'd faithfully say the same prayer over and over again.

Of death and heaven, I could think of nothing except fairies and angels, fruits and flowers that were huge and in hues beyond imagination. Of a dazzling sun and a place with no pain and no tears.

I recall a time when an argument ensued between my mother and another member of my family. I had asked my Nainamma, 'When are you going to die?' She laughed and said, 'I don't know, but I am waiting for God to take me.' This family member overheard this and informed my parents. My mom questioned me, 'Why did you ask her this question, baby?' I replied, 'Well, Nainamma prays daily to God to take her and says that heaven is a wonderful place where grandpa and her parents are. Doesn't God grant us what we ask? Isn't that the point of saying: Ask and ye shall receive, seek and ye shall find?'

My parents were speechless. My genteel mom was distressed. She was beside herself as she said to me, '*I* am being held responsible for your mistakes. I am accused of not teaching you good manners or etiquette!' This got me thinking. How could I fault my beloved mother? When I think of her now, I can clearly see that she was nothing but wonderful and kind.

At that time, I tried to explain myself better. "But…but…Mummy, isn't heaven the place where the lion and the lamb live together in perfect harmony and do not fight with each other?' Mummy shook her head, disappointed, and told me to go to sleep. She said I was reading too much. Little did I realize then that Nainamma and my understanding of death were preparing me for the next few turbulent decades of my life.

Nainamma's quiet, unyielding strength, her undying dedication to her children and students, and her love for God are things I cling to even today. I often trotted with her to the pension office, feeling very grown up. I also accompanied her to the church, her meetings, and her friend's home in East Maredpally. She was a teacher by heart and was instrumental in my early childhood education. Besides my school work, she taught me the Bible every evening. She was a strong lady who practiced religious tolerance. She also introduced me to the world of Hindu mythology and fascinated me with several stories from the Bhagwad *Gita*. I vividly recall one such story from another epic, Mahabharata. The five Pandava brothers escape the burning wax palace that the evil Kauravas had built. Nainamma often said that Good always conquers Bad in the end. We must endeavor to be good every day, she would say, adding, 'It is like taking a shower daily.'

Another memory etched in my mind is of a poem written by Vemana, the Telugu philosopher. Translation often dilutes the import of a quote or poem, but I must share the poem's essence with you. Vemana says that even when you wash the skin of a rat for a year, it does not lose its color. Similarly, when you beat a lifeless doll and command it to speak, it will never ever speak. Wise words, indeed. I relate this to my present-day life when, all too often, people stay the same and do not change. My dad often said, 'People do not change, except in the face of a life-changing tragedy that can transform them into being bitter or change them for the better.'

Another thing he often said under different circumstances, though, was, 'Such a hypocrite!' after which, each time, he explained the meaning of this word, and we retorted, 'Yes, dad, we know, we know'! He explained that this word has its genesis in a Greek word meaning 'actor.' Looking back now, I wonder, aren't we all actors playing out our parts every day— each one leading their life and acting a part whether they like it or not?

My parents had a wonderful fairytale romance. They were related to each other. My mom hailed from a rich family, whereas my dad came from a middle-class one. Often, money was scarce in my dad's family. My dad was barely 16 when he started working to support his family. The rift between the two families continues even to this day.

I learned pretty early about the differences between my dad's and my mom's families. I am my father's daughter, and I have his strong character. At the same time, my mom's characteristics also remain with me. My mom was a beautiful person whom I held more in awe of than anything else, considering I was this thin and gawky girl. I held her in a sort of a cloud reserved for the fairies. I knew I could never be like her. She was utterly graceful, whereas I was rough on the edges and untamed. That wild streak still persists in me. I was fiery back then, and to a degree, I am fiery even now. I have inherited many of my father's characteristics, one of which is to take calculated risks. My mom considered this rather foolhardy.

My mom was an English teacher at Kendriya Vidyalaya High School in Golconda. Her calm, quiet nature and her beauty will always be remembered. She was an avid reader who instilled in me at a very early age a deep love for reading. She often counseled me and encouraged me to read every day. She said it would help me improve my English. I thought this was simply her ploy to make me read every day.

My mom completed her Master's degree after two children — my brother and I. She specialized in Greek history and told us stories of Greece and Egypt. I often thought of visiting these far-off lands. Little did I realize that I would be traveling the world on business in another twenty years or so. My mother strongly influenced my education and made important decisions regarding my schooling. She sent me to Saint George Grammar School to complete my schooling. It was one of the top schools in the city. She put me on an active reading schedule, which I later learned to love. I neglected it after marriage, with all the responsibilities of that phase of life.

I started reading at the age of five. When I was a baby, my mom would read to me. I was thus actively engaged in reading from the beginning of my life. My mom always handed me a book to keep me out of trouble. This was mainly because of my restless nature, she said. I was bored with school work, which I found to be easy. Thanks to my mother, I owned hundreds of books and accumulated a sort of mini-library over the years, well into my teens and twenties. Enid Blyton, Nancy Drew, Secret Seven, James Hadley Chase, Harold Robbins, Rabindranath Tagore, Swami Vivekananda, and many others graced my cute little bookshelf. Some classics I love are *The Pilgrim's Progress*, *The Count of Monte Cristo*, Gora, the complete works of

William Shakespeare, and the poetry of Byron, Yeats, Keats, and William Wordsworth. By the time I was fourteen, I was already into Harold Robins. AJ Cronin and Pearl S Buck. I loved *Hatter's Castle*. I studied diligently, worked hard, and busied myself with reading and studying. I made up my mind that I would be a doctor. My dad bought me four medical encyclopedias when he worked in the Middle East, which I treasured and kept close to my heart when I was 12. I remember feeling very important with these books and would pour over the medical procedures and knowledge. I knew I would be a doctor and make my parents incredibly proud.

We lived in a joint family with my Nainamma and Dad's siblings. My dad often traveled to other parts of India as a driller. When he returned home after his travels, it was such a riot! We used to flock to, ambush, and gambol all over him. He always came bearing gifts and would lift my brother and me onto his shoulders. Late nights were a thing with my parents, and late shows at the movies were always such fun! This was something Nainamma disapproved of. I was spoilt by my parents with good things in life in my early years.

Christmas was the best time of the year. I got four new sets of clothes, one each for carol singing, Christmas day, New Year and my birthday. We left the Christmas decorations on until Jan 19, my birthday, and took them down the next day. I was a pensive child who spent most of her time reading, climbing trees, or running on the wall of our compound, balancing gingerly. One of my favorite pastimes was climbing the roof while hoisting myself up a window onto a mango tree. From the mango tree, I would jump onto the shed and across the tiled part of the lower roof. From there, onto the upper part of the roof. In this day and age, this would be called child endangerment. Gone are the days when mothers chastised their kids for staying outside and playing out in the open for hours. The scenario now is entirely different; mothers worry that their children are glued to electronic devices throughout the day!

Those were happy days. I was a happy child, and my life was filled with love and laughter.

Misunderstandings crept in when some family members moved into my Nainamma's home with their children due to their strained financial situation. My parents decided to move out of my Nainamma's home. We moved to Mehdipatnam, more than an hour from her place. I missed my Nainamma a lot, cried daily, and fell sick quite often. Concerned, my parents moved back closer to Nainamma's home. I felt safe and at peace again after visiting her every day after school, in the evening, after which I went outside and spent time with my friends who lived down the street. I was a carefree bird.

Until tragedy struck.

On one such day, without any warning, we received word that Nainamma had a paralytic stroke. My world turned upside down.

She could not speak or feed herself. She was hospitalized for a lengthy period, after which she was brought home. I visited her in the hospital. When she came back to her home, I visited her every evening. She would lie on her bed without much movement. She sometimes cried, her tears streaming down her pale cheeks. She could not wipe them away since she could not lift her arms. I would feed her mashed food with a spoon and try to clean her, but she was too heavy for me to move. I wanted to nurse my Nainamma, but my frailty betrayed me.

Often, my brother helped. He helped me open her mouth to clean the food that remained stuck to the left side of her mouth since she was unable to move that part of her face. Seeing her wither in front of my eyes, my heart broke into a thousand pieces. My ears yearned for the sound of her voice calling my name. But nothing of the sort happened.

It was pitiful. *Does life have to come to this*? I thought. She had fed, clothed, and bathed me when I was younger. She had taken care of me. And here she was, robbed of speech and almost lifeless. I was helpless and sad. Seeing this courageous lady, a powerful influence on my early childhood, fall this way broke me. My brother and I visited her daily after school, but things were never the same.

Soon, Nainamma passed away. Several bed sores had eaten into her frail body.

The day she passed away was the day I felt utterly lonely, my world unsafe and broken. Seeing her body lying in that coffin was my first close encounter with the death of a loved one. My Nainamma looked peaceful and happy in her eternal sleep. Even to this day, I remember everything she taught me. I pass on the good to my children, trust them, and pray that they will pass it on to *their* children.

Seeing her lying lifeless, I felt a weight on my shoulders. My parents gave us the best of things and were working themselves to the bone day and night. Nainamma gave me and my brother precious time, something she did not give any of her other grandchildren. I am the eldest of more than 40 grandchildren, and my brother was the family's baby boy. I was my Nainamma's 'Rose of Sharon,' a name she also gave the home she bought with my grandfather. She was the only person who called me this way. My mom's brother, Chinni Uncle, is the only one in the family who still calls me the 'Rose of Sharon.' No one else uses this affectionate nickname for me.

As a child, my brother was good-looking. He inherited his good looks from my parents. He was a shy child who was very attached to Mom. He cried almost every day, early in the morning. My early memories of him are that he was cute and cried daily at around 7 am when my mom was busy making breakfast and rushing through the morning chores. He would be standing close to the almirah, leaning his frail body in the crook of the wall near the kitchen, fully dressed in his checkered blue uniform, shoes and all. And crying. 'Mommy, carry me!' My mother's attention was all he cared about. When my mom used to go about her chores, my brother used to feel neglected.

Many mornings, I was frustrated by his non-stop crying. I tried to calm him down. He was too sedate for me; I considered him docile. I tried to instill some of my reckless behavior in him. Once, I helped him climb my favorite mango tree. We were caught in the middle of a sudden thunderstorm when we were up there. My brother refused to climb down the tree for several hours as it poured, though I pleaded for him to come down. 'I'll catch you!' I said. I felt quite frustrated and fell into trouble with our neighbor, who finally came to his rescue. My brother was soaking wet. He caught a cold, and my mother scolded me for being reckless. Such fun times we had together! Both of us studied at J Faust, a prestigious school of yesteryears, until the fourth grade. He and I slowly grew apart in our teens and twenties.

And then, we were married, and each ventured to find our own paths. We reconnected again in the later part of life.

My Nainamma was the matriarch who held the family together. Once she was gone, my dad's siblings grew apart, a few relocating to Australia and the others to America and Canada. Once they were married, everyone grew apart, and we rarely met.

I grew further apart, distancing myself from everyone, drowning myself in studying and reading. We attended family get-togethers as usual during the holidays and church on Sundays. At other times, we visited our relatives. My parents were very helpful to their relatives. I busied myself, trying to get ahead in life, studying, and doing my thing, as one would say. I wanted to be a doctor and was highly focused on my education. 'Intermediate,' which is known as junior college, flew by. I passed with flying colors and began my Bachelor's degree, majoring in Biology, Zoology, and Chemistry.

My father, seeking a better life for us, left India to work in the Middle East. My mother did not want to live alone with the kids, so she moved in with her mother and siblings.

A sense of despondency crept over me. I communicated with my dad through letters. He wrote religiously. I received three letters from him every week. We wrote to each other for several years. I still have the letters he wrote me when I was 14! He was a wonderful father who loved me no matter what I did. I began to read starry-eyed romantic novels such as *Mills and Boons, Harold Robbins,* and Danielle Steele's books more than was good for me.

When I think of this now, I wonder how I lost structure and direction in life. I grew distant from my brother and my mother. We now lived with my maternal grandmother and Mom's siblings. Over time, my mom and my brother drifted apart, and we coped with whatever life threw at us. My mother was the only person who worked during that time. She was often exhausted, fending for her extended family. She left home at 7:00 am and returned at 7:00 pm on most days, taking three buses to Golconda, where she worked.

My brother and I were then in the prime of our teenage. The stage was set for us to make or break the rest of our lives. Life was now set to roll on a new trajectory. I recall my mother telling me once when I was a child and bolts of thunder hit the sky, 'Baby, don't go out in the rain.' Her warning was clear. 'Don't go out when it is thundering. The thunder god loves the firstborn. If he throws out his bolt, it never goes back to him. He will simply grab you into his arms. I cannot bring you back.' That was precisely what happened to me, except that the thunderbolt was life itself.

My father returned from the Middle East, and the strain of living in a joint family took its toll. My parents, brother, and I moved into another home nearby. I was relieved that my father was back home from his business trips. But I knew that the years after I lost my Nainamma and when my father had been abroad, would never come back.

I became more lonesome, trying to understand myself, and I grew more distant from everyone. Life had taken its toll on my little family of four. I no longer shared secrets with my father, though we did things together as a family. I grew restless. The void created by my Nainamma's absence and my father's relocation was never filled. My entire self changed for the worse. I shrank into a shell and lost my emotional attachment to everyone around me. A prolonged period of loneliness took hold of me. Perhaps it was the age of rebellion. I often took off on long solo cycling trips, racing along the parade ground strip. Sometimes, I'd go with my brother or friends. We would tear down a lonely road at breakneck speed and feel like we were Hollywood stars on motorbikes. I often cut classes and went to the movies. In short, I did what the other girls my age did.

Dr. Sharon Joshua John

My First Educational Goal Crashes

I enthusiastically completed my Intermediate (12th grade) and wrote the entrance examination to be accepted into medical school. I was utterly disappointed and angry when I didn't get through. I was a victim of the so-called caste reservation system. This caste-based reservation is prevalent in India even today. It is a quota system that provides the benefit of education to a group of people hailing from the 'lower' castes, even if they scored lower than D grade during their high school years. Such a student could get a seat in a good college while a star A+ student could not.

I did not fit the particular caste or creed of people who would benefit from this reservation. I felt angry that several of my friends who scored a D were accepted into medical school simply because they came from a particular caste that had been discriminated against hundreds of years ago. The scenario has changed drastically since then, and many people belonging to the once-downtrodden castes are now wealthy and influential. It made no sense to favor them through this reservation, I thought. I felt cheated about my dream of becoming a doctor. The competition was fierce. If you did not belong to one of the castes with a reserved seat quota, you had to be an Einstein or cough up a considerable sum of money as a donation to the college, both of which seemed an illusion to me and most people.

Coming in the wake of my Nainamma's death, this rejection sent me deeper into the abyss of despondency. I missed my Nainamma during this time but did not share my thoughts with my parents.

Disgusted with this caste-based reservation system, which was, and is prevalent in the arena of jobs, too, I thought India was not the place for me anymore. I set my sights on the United States. Both my uncles had immigrated long ago when I was a kid, one to the States and the other to Australia. My father was already well-traveled. I consoled myself that I, too, would move to the States and pursue my dream of becoming a doctor. I had heard that there was no caste or quota system for people in America, so I would never be discriminated against there. I wanted to belong to some place where everybody was treated equally. I had heard that the USA was a place where people were not judged or given extra privileges without due merit. I wanted to shine for my talent.

I did not realize then that humans are the strangest creatures on earth. Every human being discriminates; you look at someone, and your brain is wired to pass judgment immediately. No sooner do we look at someone than we assume things about them. 'Oh, he is very rich!', 'she dresses well,' 'She does not look like a good person," and the list goes on. It took me time to understand that we never know the other person's story, and it is best not to judge. However, this is a learned trait that I have trained myself to master.

Everyone assumes something about the others. Aren't they discriminating? Aren't they judging them? There is a fine line between judging and discrimination, a grey zone where one bleeds into another. Sadly, the world is still the same even now, with discrimination rampant in the USA, too — the country I have called home for more than two decades.

I told my parents about my desire to leave India.

My dad was beyond thrilled. My mom was happy that I had set a goal for myself. Though they never said they were disappointed that I wasn't accepted into medical school, I felt I had failed them. I was angry and bitter that I was forced to take another route in life. I began to feel more lost than usual. Though my parents supported, loved, and encouraged me in everything I did, I did not share my innermost thoughts with them. They thought all was well with me.

During this time of my life, the monotonous laboratory work and the lectures did not interest me. I joined the Bachelor's program specializing in Botany, Zoology, and Chemistry at Kasturba Gandhi College, Secunderabad. I thought everything lacked meaning and purpose and that my life was lackluster. I was bored with my education; it seemed too easy. I was distracted and often accompanied my peers to the movies in the afternoon. I'd then return home, racing on my bicycle to reach home on time. Even if I missed classes, I quickly caught up with my studies. Somehow, the hand of the Almighty was upon me, favoring me with a good memory and a firm grasp of subjects. I took this as a reaffirmation that I was indeed the 'Rose of Sharon.' In the final exams, I scored an A+ and topped my class.

We students often wasted time sitting in the park adjacent to Kasturba Gandhi College. We'd sit watching the passersby, poking fun at them, or eating street food from a bandi which is a street cart.

I began reading romantic novels more, apart from Khalil Gibran, my mother's favorite author. I do think the inevitable happened to me. When one is fed by an overdose of Gibran, one must become illogical. I truly believe I became a hopeless romantic, with a desire to be loved till 'death do us part.' I read more of my mom's books, burying myself deep into the works of Greek history, which my mother had studied for her Master's degree. I was in a true state of 'excess of knowledge is vexation to the spirit.' I read other books, too, perhaps a little too much for my age, when I should have been focused on getting accepted into medical school.

A Meeting with Destiny

During this period of my life, I was going through a personal crisis. The strain of living in a joint family was taking its toll on my untamed spirit. We were back to living in a joint family with my maternal grandmother and my mom's siblings. Everything seemed so difficult. Simple things such as taking a shower with two buckets of water would be deemed a waste of water. Use of the gas stove would be a waste of gas. Touching the refrigerator was not allowed, and speaking too loudly was rude. Sitting on the sofa was not allowed; rushing from room to room was forbidden. My mom, my brother, and I were asked to live in one room; other parts of the house were off-limits. Later on, Dad returned from the Gulf and started sharing this room with us.

We were not allowed to use the main bathroom and had to walk a long way to use another one, which was tiny. We were not allowed into the kitchen but, instead, were asked to cook in a tiny adjacent room that had a sink. We had to cook, bathe, and wash clothes in the same sink, which was technically neither a kitchen nor a bathroom. Using certain plates or certain glasses was forbidden. Sitting on my grandmother's or aunt's beds was not allowed. With all these restrictions, one can imagine the kind of claustrophobic life I was living. This was the absolute opposite of my life in Nainamma's home, where I had shared her bed, warm blanket, and whatever else I wanted.

These, although trivial, endless daily troubles irritated and frustrated me repeatedly. Being the way they wanted me to and adopting a very restrained demeanor was beyond my capacity. Curiously, my mom, brother, and dad did not seem to mind this. I had been a wild child while growing up in

Maredpally with my Nainamma, who had nurtured me as a child and taught me the right things. I had spent half of my holidays on the street playing hopscotch or Seven Stones and running around wildly. When the sun was too hot, I would indulge in a good read. The nuances of behaving in a modest, girly way were foreign to me. They stifled my spirit. I grew rebellious by the minute.

My father counseled me to be patient. On the other hand, my mother, who could deal with my boisterous behavior, most often let me be myself. I greatly appreciated this. She equipped me with the skills required to live a good life. My parents never chastised me at any time during my formative years. They led by example, were extremely generous, and were role models to the other members of the family, often supporting them financially and morally. In fact, they had sponsored several family weddings, funerals, hospital bills, food and shelter for others, and never saved anything for their golden years.

In the midst of all this strife, I continued to miss my Nainamma terribly. I was restless and turned to God for help. I sought solace in prayer. I was the poster child to my parents, yet I was troubled and disturbed. I wasn't sure where my life was headed. I was letting myself wander and fall into some sort of abyss of confusion, though, from the outside, I appeared to be poised since I excelled at studies and sports and avidly took part in extra-curricular activities. I told myself that, at that time in life, I needed a Plan B and a Plan C to survive. *I must start anew and search for a better focus in life*, I told myself.

I began to live and breathe Khalil Gibran and entered a world of fantasy. I felt rather intoxicated. Gibran was a Lebanese-American writer, poet, and visual artist. He is the author of

The Prophet, which continues to inspire the young and the old even today. *The Prophet* was published in 1923 and has been released in more than 20 languages.

What I loved about Gibran were his philosophical and inspirational essays. His writings were deeply emotional; he spoke of love, marriage, children, joy, sorrow, crime, punishment, freedom, reason, passion, pain, self-knowledge, teaching, friendship, time, good, evil, prayer, pleasure, beauty, religion, and death. He kept it real, and the emotions he talked about were real, too. Every human experiences them. But strangely, the essays and poems that *really* drew me to him were those on powerful love, death, and pain. This may seem illogical to some because of my scientific background and the fact that I have authored several scientific papers. At work, I am a person who has a purpose and objective, uses scientific methods, and achieves precise results. I carefully tie back the conclusion to the objectives. Everything needs structure in science; everything has a reason and rationale. Everything in medicine, too, needs evidence. In spite of this stark reality, I look back with fond memories of that innocent phase of my life when I seemed to be in a dream.

I look back to the moment when I fell in love. What was that? Love? Yes! Love, that so-called chemical reaction of dopamine pumping into my blood, sending shivers down my spine. I don't know what happened to me, and I still haven't figured it out. That moment, when I first set my eyes on Andy, was magical. I never felt that way again, even with Andy himself, especially after he broke my heart barely within a year of our marriage. I never recovered from that blow.

My adrenaline spiked to dangerous levels. Adrenaline, that rouge 3F flight, fight, and fright hormone I had read about in my textbook on Endocrinology — the hormone that made me blush and sweat and made my heart race. I was a ticking time bomb waiting to be blown to smithereens by love. Gibran's words on wisdom and love kept me on the edge and in anticipation that love would come flying around the corner and rescue me from the weight of existence. And boy, did it come flying into my life!

It was a warm March afternoon. I was racing back home on my blue bicycle after attending my laboratory class in the final year of my Bachelor's degree at Kasturba Gandhi College. I found laboratory work and dissections fascinating and religiously attended them from 8 am to 10 am every day, almost like clockwork. After the lab classes were over, I rarely attended the lectures that went on till a little after noon. I would often hang out outside the college campus, gobbling paani puri, a street food popular in many parts of India, from the carts lined up along the street. Or, I'd spend time with my friends. Sometimes, we caught the 11 am movie, hung out at a nearby park, or had coffee at a friend's home while listening to music.

My dad often cautioned me not to race around on my bicycle. He would say if I owned a motorbike, it would not be able to control my rough handling! I loved the rush of the wind passing through my hair as I raced along the streets on my cycle. I imagined that I was actually riding a Harley, like in one of those Western movies my parents often took us to.

That warm March afternoon, flying home gaily on my bicycle, I reached a junction close to my college. All of a sudden, a dashing young man came out of nowhere on his motorcycle, revving his engine. I remember the scene vividly even now. His Java had a tinted windshield with three brilliant silver stars on it. He abruptly stopped his motorbike in front of my bicycle. Smack!! Right in the middle of the street. Completely taken by surprise, I swerved sharply, almost falling off my bicycle, trying to avoid what could have been a major accident. I was terribly shaken; all I could think of was broken bones and my upcoming exams.

Thankfully, nothing was broken. *Phew!*

When I look back at those few moments, I wonder whether the fact that this literally happened at the crossroads was a metaphor and a portent of what was to come in my life. I did not realize then that those few minutes of my life were heavily symbolic. I was to take a U-turn in life; the entire course of my destiny was to change in the next few months in ways I can't fully comprehend to this day.

I often talk to my children about this encounter and challenge them that while life does give us a second chance, it does not return the time that has passed. One *can* change some things, but one can never turn the clock back. Every minute counts — *tick tock tick tock*...the clock keeps ticking on. Some decisions can break you yet make you stronger, bigger, and better. I sometimes think to myself wryly, 'Yes! I *did* take the road less traveled.

I was more in shock than anger when this stranger barred my path, stopping his motorbike in the middle of the street in front of my bicycle with a boyish smile. I did not understand this audacity and confidence. Before I could gather my wits and address this brazen behavior, he said, 'Hello! How are you?' It took me a moment to realize that he was asking me. Gathering my wits somewhat, I replied, 'I am fine. Do you need to speak to someone?' I was taken further aback when he said, 'Yes, you.'

My eyes widened, and I shot out, 'What!'

I had no idea what he wanted from me. An impish grin dancing on his face, he repeated, 'Yes, you.'

'What is it you want?' I needed to know.

What he said next threw me totally off guard. 'Do you want to go out for coffee at Nandita ice cream parlor?'

Contrary to my normal response of rudely refusing when someone asked me out, I did not say no to him. I don't know what came over me. All I managed to mumble was, 'No, I cannot, not now. My exams are coming up in the next two weeks, and I need to focus on them.' I was such a good girl!

Before he could say anything else, I picked up my fallen bicycle, jumped onto it, all flustered, and took off like a bullet.

The next minute, he was following me at a safe distance!

I kept my head down and pedaled furiously back home. I threw my bicycle at the entrance and ran inside. I ran to my window to see him speeding away. My heart was pounding wildly. *What had happened*, I wondered. I recalled that I had seen him before. In the past two months, he had been coming, almost every second day, to where we girls hung out. He was actually interested in having a coffee with me! My inability to vocalize my thoughts during that three-minute exchange was something I could not understand. Nor could I understand why this young man would be interested in me. I was just a regular girl on a bicycle!

All at once, it dawned on me that I was thinking of this stranger who did not know my name. And whose name *I* didn't know. It seemed incredible since it was not a true image of myself. I spent a restless night thinking of our conversation and my reaction to his overture. Over and over, the scene kept playing in my mind. My heart lurched every time I recalled his sentences. And the simple 'You' that he uttered when I asked him who he wanted to speak to. That 'You' was enough to make me mentally reel and swoon. Lying in my bed, I saw stars; my head was in pink fluffy clouds. It was early morning by the time I drifted off into sleep.

The next day, I took extra care in dressing. Jumping onto my bicycle, I raced to college, all the time watching to see if I was being followed by *him*. This 'taking extra care while dressing' went on for almost three weeks. I did not see him again. I went through a spectrum of emotions: happy, sad, upset, angry, and then feeling played. I had no idea what was happening. I even wondered if my encounter with him had been a dream. It had been a barely three-minute conversation with a complete stranger. And yet, it had stirred up so many emotions in me. Being a focused, level-headed young lady, I told myself that I was turning prematurely senile.

For some strange reason, I thought of Mary Brodie in AJ Cronin's *Hatters Castle.* Such a random thought! In the story, Mary is a studious, obedient daughter. I was a studious and obedient daughter, too. I aced my grades at college, participated in activities, and was extremely good at athletics. I was my dad's and Mom's darling little all-rounder, the girl Dad often referred to as 'first in class, from KG (kindergarten) to PG (post-graduation).'

I did not share the 'boy incident,' as I called it then, with any of my friends. I began to earnestly study for my pre-final examinations that were around the corner. But deep down, I was sad. A strange restlessness crept over me.

Three weeks later, when I thought this entire incident had been a prank, I saw him standing by his motorbike, waiting for me at the entrance to my college. He waved at me. I gingerly crossed the street, righteously emboldened by his disappearance over the past three weeks. I could not help myself and asked him, 'Hey! Where have you been all these days?'

He replied, 'Oh! You said you had exams. I wanted to give you a break to study.' Trust me, I thought that was the best pickup line in history, but I have never heard of it and probably will never hear of that pickup line. That simple reply made the adrenaline rush through my veins and into my head. He actually valued my studies and my intention to become a better person!

That was a defining moment for me.

My First Date

He invited me to go with him to Nandita ice cream parlor, a ten-minute ride, for coffee and snacks. We still did not know each other's names. Not that I cared. By now, I had thrown caution and reasoning out the window. Parking my bicycle at the bicycle stand at college, I hopped onto his motorbike. We went to Nandita to have ice cream and snacks. When I got off the motorbike, he laughingly said, 'We don't even know each other's names!' I said, 'true! And here I am, with a stranger. You could be a killer. You could kill me and throw me into some ravine.' This made him laugh heartily. What a laugh it was! I was mesmerized.

He introduced himself as Andy, and I replied, 'Sharon.' We had a decent conversation, exchanging pleasantries and talking about what he did and my forthcoming final exams. All the time, I kept looking at him carefully, finding that his eyes were holding me captive. I felt like I had known him for ages.

Andy asked me to meet him again the next Sunday. I said I could not. In any case, I rarely went out on weekends with my friends. He said, 'Let's meet on Saturday.' I was very nervous that someone would see us together on his motorbike and report it to my dad.

We spoke about many things. He seemed to enjoy watching and listening to me. I talked and talked like there was no tomorrow. I did not know that he was sizing me up, hardly paying any attention to most of the things I said. He told me that he had a college degree and was working as a manager in the state government's road transport company. It was three years into my marriage with him when I came to know the truth regarding his education and designation at work. I clearly remember that day. While browsing through some old documents, I found out that he was a high-school dropout. The discovery devastated me. I realized with shock that while I had always shared everything about my life with him from the beginning, he had not reciprocated. He had not only concealed the truth from me but also *lied* to me blatantly. I felt betrayed.

Anyway, back to the ice cream parlor and our first date. I did not know that his interests were different from mine. Perhaps he had never met my type in his 27-odd years; he was much older than me. I told him that my interests lay in movies, music, and lots of other stuff, other than mainly academics. I remember one sentence of his vividly from that conversation. He said, 'You're really a good girl, right?' I thought he was being funny and didn't realize that he really meant it. Later, I would come to know that he was a philandering young man who knew the right words to use with every kind of girl he met. I remember replying, 'What do you mean? Yes, I am a good girl. I like to study.' You see, in my world, being good meant getting good grades in school and college. Call me naïve, but that was how I was at that age.

We set up another date for the following Saturday. He said, 'This time, we'll be going with a group of friends to Gandipet.' Gandipet was a desolate place, almost two hours away from Hyderabad. It was a picnic spot with a lake.

After almost two hours at the ice cream parlor, Andy dropped me back at the college, and I rushed back home. Luckily, my parents were at work. I quietly went about my studies and routine chores as if nothing had happened.

The Second Date

I had not said 'no' when Andy had invited me to the picnic the following Saturday. Instead, I was scheming about informing my parents that I would be gone an entire Saturday. I had never done that in all my years! My life had been at my college, library, and, on rare occasions, visiting other relatives. I had studied in an all-girls school and been accepted into an all-girls college. My life was governed by structure. More importantly, on Saturdays, I dedicated more time to studying.

Any other time I went out unless it was college, I was accompanied by my parents or my brother. My parents would never have it — me going with a bunch of boys and girls to visit the outskirts of the city. It seemed taboo but fun; girls with good grades simply didn't do that sort of thing. But under all those good grades, I was a rebel; no one quite understood me.

Before the trip to Gandipet, Andy and I met again at the same ice cream parlor. I asked him, 'How many people are going on this outing? All girls or all boys or…?' I left the sentence hanging in mid-air. There was something about his eyes. He looked at me strangely, but I did not find it odd.

'Well,' he explained, 'I did tell my friends you're my girlfriend, and yes, there will be boys *and* girls.' I instantly loved his assertiveness. I giggled and said, 'Your girlfriend? Really?! We don't even know each other properly.' I felt antiquated. Now, when I look back at that old self of mine, I don't know whether it was being innocent or foolish. Instead of being skeptical about Andy, I actually tried to warn him about *me*. Little did I know that I should have been worried about myself and not the other way around. Well, never mind, I can't turn back the clock.

Andy's eyes bore into mine as he said, 'I know you're good, and that is all that matters.' Oh, well! He always said the right thing at the right time! I instantly felt a warmth rise in my chest. I looked outside. It was getting late. I had never stayed out of home after sunset. It was a rule at home. I panicked and told Andy, 'I must leave now, or I will be in trouble at home. The sun has set.' He sounded incredulous. 'What! You mean, you can't stay out after sunset. You're joking, right?' I said, No, I am not joking; I am dead serious."

I explained the situation at home in great detail. He guffawed insolently. That made me blush in embarrassment. I do feel ancient now as I write these lines about curfew time and the unwritten rule of having to be back home before sunset. In the years since then, everything has changed. Not many young people have a curfew time today. But that was then, and that was India; the 'good girls' had to adhere to several rules.

Andy said, 'Come on, Sharon, you're a big girl now! Why don't we go for a ride down Tivoli Road?' This made me a bit nervous because I heard it was a lonely part of the city. Not many people ventured there in the dark. And ghosts were supposed to lurk around that place! I stammered, 'Really? But why?' *Funny*, I think to myself now, *I was out of high school and in college and still believed in ghosts*! Indeed, it was rather quaint even back then.

Andy had this weird habit of throwing questions back at me instead of replying to mine. True to this habit, he responded with, 'Why not?'

I fidgeted with my dress as I searched for the right words. 'We could be accosted by a ghost or two. I've heard stories about this road, and that would mean I cannot go back home.' I said this in all sincerity. His reaction was incomprehensible. He laughed. Laughed really hard for a good two minutes, tears in his eyes.

'I never thought you could be so naïve. This makes you more attractive.'

'Well, I am serious!'

'As long as I am with you, no ghost or devil can come close to you.'

The right words, indeed, the right words! I was mesmerized by his charm and interest in me that day, too, and enamored at hearing the right words at the right time. *He is something*, I thought. Andy persuaded me, 'Come on, this will be a fun ride. We could even race down the road without the cops tailing us.' Finally, I agreed and said, 'Okay, let's do this!'

And off we went to Tivoli Road on his motorcycle.

We raced down the road, laughing and being silly. It was thrilling to be the pillion rider! When I returned home, I was obviously nervous, trying to think of an explanation for the delay. Luckily, my parents weren't home, only my mom's mom. I quickly snuck in and changed my clothes, feeling invigorated, and began to study. I pretended that nothing had happened. I felt extremely guilty, though, and went to bed before my parents returned home. My parents never questioned my going out — where or what. They implicitly trusted me not to do the so-called 'wrong things' in life.

Andy said he was working in another district and couldn't meet me until next Saturday. I chirpily went about my week, waiting for Saturday to come. I had to concoct a story for my parents; Andy said we would be leaving at 8 am and returning by 5 pm.

I told my mom I would be out all Saturday; I was joining some others for a college outing. My Mom seemed surprised since I had never gone on such an outing with any of my college friends. In fact, I was pretty aloof and mostly stayed to myself. I told her I would be back by 5 pm at the latest. Thankfully, she didn't ask me where we were going. There was no way she would allow me to go to Gandipet! Aside from the fact that it was a lonely place, the lake there was known to be treacherous; it had swallowed several people who had gone swimming there. The place did not have lifeguards. Those days, most parents would not allow their youngsters to go to Gandipet unaccompanied by older people. Today, I laugh, thinking of the scary stories we had heard about Gandipet.

Saturday came. I woke up at 6 am and was ready by 7.30. I took my bicycle and left to meet Andy. He had told me I could park my bicycle at his friend's pad and had given me the address. I met his friends and their girlfriends there, and we went in two cars. It took us a good 2 hours to reach our destination. On the way, I had too much to eat. We listened to loud music, hung out at the lake, and basked in the warm sunshine. The entire day was spent with laughter, love, and friends. Ah, such a carefree and happy life!

At around 3.30 pm, anxiousness began to set in. I asked Andy nervously, 'When are we going back? I have to be home by 5:00, or at the latest by 6:00. Otherwise, I will be in big trouble.' Andy seemed to be a bit irritated. He retorted, 'It's just 3.30 pm! What is the rush?' Soon, it was 4.00 pm. By this time, I was beside myself with worry. Two of Andy's friends had wandered away to a nearby café, and everyone was enjoying themselves, except for me. The rest of the evening was filled with distress. I wanted to go back home, but it was too far away from the city for me to go alone. Nor did I have enough money to take a cab.

Finally, we left at 10 pm in the night. My agitation had peaked to dread. It would be nearly 1 am by the time I reached home. I would have to take my bicycle and then go home. I had never been alone that late in the night in all those years unless you considered the late-night movie shows I'd gone to with my parents. I was filled with a sense of foreboding. My mind was full of thoughts about my dad's anger and my mom's tension. We did not have a phone at home, and there was no way I could inform them that I would be late. Angry with myself, I got into an argument with Andy.

Both of us sat in stony silence on the way back. I started crying. His friends did not think much of this. Later on, I would learn that most of them were older than me and were working; they did not have a curfew time at home. They reassured me and said they would talk to my parents, which was more fearful than *not* talking to my parents.

I was studying in a girl's college. I had lied to my parents about the outing. I had never lied to them before. This was the first time my parents would be angry at me. As for my dad, I could imagine that he would have worked himself into a rage. I wasn't sure how to handle this situation.

In the end, rather desperately, I agreed to let Andy and his friends accompany me home and inform my parents that the car had broken down or something and that we had been heavily delayed. I would pick up my bicycle the next day.

As expected, we reached my home at around 1 am. As the car neared home, I could see my parents standing at the gate with other members of the extended family. Andy did not seem anxious or upset, which shocked me. His face was expressionless; he appeared indifferent. Approaching my family, he introduced himself. 'Uncle, Aunty, my name is Andy. I am Sharon's friend. She came with us on an outing to Gandipet. We are very sorry it's late; the car broke down on the way.' My dad was livid. These were people he had never met in his entire life. He started shouting immediately, scaring me to death. I had never seen him so angry or shout at me. When he had shouted at all, it had always been directed at others. I think the possibility that something bad could have happened to me had shaken him thoroughly.

Dad asked Andy, 'Who are you? I don't know you. I don't need to address your impertinence. Be respectful of who you are speaking with.' There it was, the first encounter between Andy and Dad. The dislike was mutual and immediately palpable. That mutual anger and dislike continued for years until Dad became tolerant towards his son-in-law. This was almost 15 years into my marriage with Andy. Probably, Dad softened a bit, knowing that I would never leave Andy until death literally parted us.

My dad refused to speak to anyone. He marched me into the house and shut the door. I was shattered, because the poster child image of mine had been destroyed. Disappointment was written all over my dad's face. He began questioning me. 'Who are these people?' He knew a few girlfriends of mine, but there had been all new faces today. 'Who is this, Andy? He does not seem right; he looks like a thug. I am ashamed of you.' This went on and on.

After a point, I could not stand it anymore. I told him, 'Dad, I really like him. Please don't speak about him like this.' That was it; all hell broke loose. It was nothing short of a battle. My mother was silent most of this time. I think she was more shocked than angry. That night, I cried myself to sleep. I woke up in the morning and realized I'd have no bicycle that day. I told my dad, 'I have to go get my bicycle.' He said there was no need to go to college that day. He wanted the address of the place where I had parked my bicycle. I gave it to him.

I stayed at home the entire day and cried.

Ready to be Married!

I did not see Andy for another fortnight. He worked in another district, which was a good three-hour bus journey away. I got busy studying for my final examinations. My parents watched my movements very carefully, and the others at home were vigilant as well. I wasn't allowed to go anywhere unaccompanied; it was awful. My dad began to accompany me to college and stayed at the gate until the end of the day. He did not take up another drilling contract but remained in Hyderabad. I could not miss any of my classes, use my bicycle, or eat paani puri. I felt chained, which made me angrier than ever. I did not tell any of my friends in college what had transpired; they were puzzled at the change they saw come over me. In any case, I wasn't close to any girlfriends I hung out with, so they did not think much of it. In fact, come to think of this, I truly had no best friend. Just acquaintances during my college days.

Studying was a big part of my life. I continued attending college with a heavy heart while preparing for my exams. Earlier, I used to sit on my window sill and study. But now, I was banned from doing that, too. Just before the exams, we had a holiday week to prepare; college was closed.

Andy did not find me in college. It was the third week I had not seen him. I heard a knock on my door at around 1 pm one day. My grandmother was sleeping. My mom had gone to school, and my dad wasn't home either. I opened the door to find Andy on my doorstep. My heart almost stopped. I said, 'Andy! My dad will kill you or me if he finds you here. You'd best leave.' He was unperturbed. He was actually amused, I think. He said, 'I really like you, Sharon, and have fallen in love with you and your innocence. I want to marry you.' I was utterly confused. I realized later that this was the moment when he had proposed to me. At the doorstep of my home, both of us stood on different sides of the threshold. How incredible this sounds! And yet true. I met him around three times and was ready to be married. I had also first met him at the crossroads.

I did not know what to make of it. I think his reckless behavior was immensely appealing to me at that time. He persisted and asked me, 'Do you want to marry me or not?' Almost demanding an immediate answer. It all felt strange, like I was in a movie. I said, 'Andy, I am going to have my final examinations next week; this would be disruptive. If you want to marry me, you will have to speak to my parents and ask them for my hand. This can happen, after I complete my exams.'

Promising me that he would be back with his mom and dad and that they would speak to my parents, he left. I felt much at peace and was able to study. Most importantly, I was able to keep this secret safe with me until my exams were over.

A Month in Orissa

Andy had proposed, and I had accepted. I was immensely attracted to his fearlessness; I found it terribly appealing. I was energized, knowing I would soon be married to the love of my life. Strangely, my focus on my studies sharpened because I knew I would soon be taking a plunge into a future of love and would live happily ever after. I am not sure if I had lost my voice of reason or whether I was still utterly disappointed at not being accepted to medical school.

Suffused in the light of love, I finished my exams. I thought I did them well. A few days after that, Andy came home as promised, bringing his mom along. It was a Sunday afternoon. My parents were home. Obviously, they were terribly surprised and angry to see both mother and son at our doorstep. My heart, on the contrary, was singing. I believed Andy was doing the right thing by asking my parents for my hand in marriage. Expectedly, my dad was furious; my parents thought this was rude and unconventional and did not like it at all. They detested the idea of my marrying a Hindu, not understanding their ancestors were Hindus themselves.

They expressed their displeasure immediately.

To this, Andy said, 'Uncle, I really like your daughter and want to marry her. I am willing to convert to Christianity and get married in a church.' After that, there was a lot of formal talk, with my parents grilling Andy and his mom. How many siblings did he have, where was their native place, what did his family members do, and did Andy have a job? Through it all, Dad sat there fuming, seething with rage. Finally, he spat out these words to Andy, 'You're not worthy of my daughter. How dare you come here like this, uninvited? Is this the correct way? You people have no culture. Where is your father, why didn't he come?' On and on it went.

Andy and his mom got up, saying it was not right for them to be insulted. They left in a huff. My mom and dad were furious with me. Then began the shouting. I received an earful about being involved with this 'thug.' I, too, was furious and began to argue with them. We got into a shouting match, which shocked my parents. I had always been docile and a 'proper girl,' remember? And this frustrated them to no end.

The next day, Dad left with Mom and me for his next drilling project in Orissa. My summer holidays had begun. The results of the final exam would be out in two months. Amidst a lot of pain, tears, and anger, I accompanied my parents on this trip. We stayed in my dad's manager's home; it was sheer hell, with nothing to do the entire day. I had no books to read or bicycle and was worried that Andy would look for me in Hyderabad and not find me.

My dad's manager said he would allow me to stay in Orissa and continue studying there. I wasn't prepared to stay there since Mom would return home soon when her summer holidays ended. There were several things she had to tend to in Hyderabad. I refused to eat and stayed silent the entire time, sunk in melancholy. My parents were distraught to see me like this, and my dad decided to send me back to Hyderabad with my mom. He made me promise that I would continue to study and would not meet Andy. I promised him, but this was because I wanted to return home. I was willing to say anything to leave Orissa. I found that a terrible place to live in. Hyderabad was home, a vibrant and happening place.

I breathed a sigh of relief when our train reached Hyderabad. I was chastised enough and decided I was over with boy talk and marriage and all that foolishness. I was confined to my home. I did none of the things I generally used to do, and I thought that Andy might not want to do anything with me anymore since he and his mom had been insulted by my parents. I was depressed and remained sad most of the time. I watched TV all day and did not read anything at all; I seemed to have forgotten my favorite habit. I tried to pray but found that I could not focus. I sulked most of the time.

I hadn't seen Andy for almost a month and a half, and it was mid-May now. One lovely Tuesday, when a family member and I were walking back home, Andy came on his motorbike. This family member thought he was handsome. She hadn't seen him before. Thankfully, she did say she wouldn't tell my parents about my meeting him that day.

I was beyond thrilled that I could share the joyful news with someone that I had found the love of my life, the love who had not given up on me. Andy was sad at my prolonged absence. He asked me where I had been, adding that he had searched high and low for me in college, the library, and my other haunts. And in my neighborhood. I cried to him, 'Andy, my parents took me to Orissa. They made me promise I would never meet you again. I don't know what to do!'

Andy said he understood but wanted to know why my dad hated him. I said, 'Oh! I don't know for sure, but I feel the major problem is that you're a Hindu and I, a Christian.' Why is it that most Christians discriminate against Hindus so deeply in India and even in the United States? I still fail to understand even in this modern day and age. And, of course, my dad had big dreams for me — that I would be in the United States, married off to a rich man, and all that. I was terrified of displeasing him since he thought the world of me.

I met Andy again the following week when I was with the same family member. Andy told me not to bring this person along whenever we were to meet. By now, my parents thought I had forgotten Andy, that I was studying to go to America, and that things were back to normal. They became a little more trusting and allowed me to go to the library, my favorite haunt. My dad returned from Orissa after completing his contract. He said he may go back again in August that year.

We were now in mid-June. The next time I met Andy, I did not take that family member along. I told her that Andy wanted me to meet him alone. I left in the afternoon and returned by 6 pm, my curfew time. Seated outside the home were my parents. I knew this wasn't a good sign and tried to walk past them into the house casually. My dad stopped me and asked me to sit down. 'We need to talk,' he said. I instantly knew what had happened. This family member, whom I had trusted so deeply, had informed my parents about my seeing Andy. I realized that my dad's disappointment was more terrible than his anger. It would have been better if he had yelled and raged at me. I could have somehow taken it, bad as it would have surely been. But his cold manner was worse. It weighed heavily upon me, like a block of ice on my chest.

I went to sleep that night without any peace in my heart, feeling betrayed. I thought I could convince my parents since Andy had said that he would convert to Christianity to marry me. His religion was the biggest obstacle for my parents. At this time in my life, I want to address that religion is a personal choice. I do not believe in conversion for the sake of marriage or that people should be forced to convert. Every person has been created by God, and to each his own. If you are born into a certain religion, then it is natural that you follow that path since you are taught by your parents. When I grew older, I realized that true religion did not harm anyone deliberately, either through thought, word, or deed. India has been deeply divided since forever based on caste and religion. Even after decades of an inter-caste marriage, I faced and still face hostility from the extended side of the family rather than my husband's side of the family, but that is a different topic altogether. Little did I realize that my dad was already set in his mind that Andy was the wrong choice for me. His bias against Andy, beyond the matter of religion, seemed illogical. Perhaps it was because Andy was rough and wild, unlike my family members. Or perhaps it was because my dad wanted me, his little princess, to marry someone wealthy, sophisticated, and 'well-settled.' Oh, how I hate this term!

His dislike of Andy bordered on hatred, and it continued even after I had had two children and moved to America. I often had terrible arguments with my beloved father that I would never leave Andy, no matter what happened. I understood late in life that my dad wanted me to have a normal, happy life with children and a wonderful family in the conventional sense. But by then, it was too late. I was deeply entrenched in everything and found it harder than before to walk out of my marriage to Andy. Instead, I did not want to leave him but wanted to make it work until he changed. And yes, he did change. But it took years and years, and the intervening events took a heavy toll on me, the after-effects of which I still endure.

How we women think that things will change for the better! That our men will change for the better! I always fail to understand this, though I am guilty of thinking this way. I have come across many intelligent, accomplished, yet naïve and trusting women like I was at that stage of my life. Women always think, 'My love for him will change him.' And they seem rather surprised, just like me, when 'he' does not change—or worse, changes for the worse. The man, on the other hand, thinks, 'Well, you knew me and all of this before you married me. So why do you complain now? Just deal with it.' And the vicious cycle of unhappiness continues. This happens in so many marriages across the world! And vice versa; the man harbors certain expectations from the woman and finds himself disappointed.

I have found that it is rare for a man or a woman to change for the better. And, even if such a change occurs, it happens after the other person has paid an enormous price. Much of the damage cannot be undone. The time lost will never return; the prime of one's youth is gone, never to return, no matter how much money one has. One must, therefore, choose wisely. But then, as they say, marriages are made in heaven. Or are they?

I continued studying as usual. It was my escape from the physical pain I felt in my heart. My life had certainly changed since March of my final year in college when I was studying for my bachelor's degree. It was at a point of no return. Nor did I *want* it to return to where it had been in February that year.

When I thought of Andy or was with him, I felt life was simply wonderful — carefree, like it had been when I was younger. I felt I could conquer the world and fly like an eagle. Andy was very direct and open in his feelings for me.

He was forthright in saying that he was keen to get married to me and to only me. He really wanted to do the right thing, he said. I felt loved, seen, and, more importantly, protected. This was a passion I did not experience in life again. When I see loveless and unhappy marriages, despite the presence of material wealth, I realize that, amidst everything I underwent, it is better to have loved and lost than never to have loved at all. Love is a very powerful emotion that makes us human.

During the weekends, when he was back in town, Andy rode his motorbike, revved it, and zipped past my home. This made my dad furious; he often rushed out and tried to accost Andy with a hockey stick, thinking that he could give him a thrashing. Andy thought it was hilarious, revved up his engine, and raced away, taunting my dad. I felt helpless but excited, knowing that Andy was somewhere around and had not forgotten me. One day, I mustered enough courage to call one of his friends and ask him to tell Andy to meet me on a weekday, as I had to speak to him urgently. I said I would call this friend again to tell him when and where Andy would meet me. I called him back two days later and told him that I would meet Andy the following Wednesday afternoon at our favorite rendezvous.

Wednesday came, and I left home on my bicycle without telling anyone. I sped away to Nandita Ice Cream Parlor, where Andy and I had gone on our first date — well, a date of sorts, at least. He was waiting for me. It was around 2 pm in the afternoon.

I Elope!

I was overjoyed to see Andy. We sat down and talked. I said, 'Andy, Dad is planning to get me married, and I am not even sure to whom! He thinks I am getting out of control. I see no future at home, Andy. Let's elope!'

It was now Andy's turn to be speechless.

I sensed his shock but plunged right on. 'This is the best thing for us. If you still want to marry me, this is the only option we have. Of course, if you don't want to elope and marry me, it's absolutely fine. But this will be our last meeting; I will go home and listen to my dad.'

Andy didn't say anything. He continued looking at me in shock.

I went on. 'Everyone in my family and the neighbors look at me as if I have committed a crime. I cannot stand this anymore, Andy; I don't understand this at all, and all in the family say, 'You're a Hindu, why! I feel disgusted; all of us are first human beings, and religion is secondary. I feel chained. Now that I have completed my Bachelor's degree, I want to study further, but I am sitting at home, doing nothing! I can't even go to the library. I want to be a doctor.'

My face was flushed as the words and emotions came tumbling out.

Andy held my hand and asked me, 'Are you sure about this? Because once you leave home, there will be no turning back.' Perhaps it was more of a question than a statement. I held on to his steely gaze and replied, tears in my eyes. 'Yes, I know there will be no turning back. This is what I want.' He agreed immediately, and his tone turned brisk as he said,

'I will tell my parents and siblings. We can get married in court. You will see, your parents will accept us eventually, and we will live happily. I am not a bad person. I can take care of you and keep you happy, Sharon.'

I wasn't really listening to him. I was too busy blinking through my tears and being angry with my parents for taking me to Orissa for over a month. That had made me defiant; I felt I was being controlled and shepherded according to their desire. By then, I was a completely untamed young woman who had lost all sense of reason and knew no boundaries. Growing up, both my parents had let me do whatever I wanted — maybe because, most of the time, I anyway did the conventionally right thing. I was a 'good girl' who did what most parents wanted their kids to do: go to school, study, wake up early, help at home, and be respectful and obedient. A poster child, like I said earlier. However, I did all this willingly since I wanted to do it; nobody forced me. I was a girl with a wild heart and steely determination who did not care for restraint or convention.

Andy and I decided on a date; I would leave home on July 3. We were thinking of our convenience. He had to take time off from work and come back to town for at least 2 or 3 weeks. He gave me clear instructions not to bring any gold or money from my parents' home. He said, 'Your dad could lodge a complaint with the police if you do that. I see you wear two fine gold necklaces.' I nodded and asked him, 'What about my clothes?'

'Just the ones you are wearing. I will buy you new clothes.' Once again, I felt the warmth rising in my chest. I was doing the right thing, and things would work out fine in the end.

For a long time, especially after my Nainamma had passed, I had been feeling repressed in our joint family, with its daily irritations. As both my parents were the only working members of the joint family, they became de facto parents to the others in the family, too, and I felt neglected. The only time I had felt safe was when my parents had lived with my Nainamma in Maredpally. When she died, everything started falling apart for me. My dad was a hardworking man who worked and traveled a lot to put food on the table. When he was home, he spent a lot of time with my brother and I. My mom, too, was very hardworking. She provided for our family at all times, taking care of the others as well. She had a hard life and was quite frail. As for me, I was an uncut diamond those days, still rough around the edges. It, therefore, took my breath away when I found a man who made me feel that I was the most beautiful girl in the world. I felt I was being seen. I did tell Andy it was important that I continue to study and complete my post-graduation since my career was going to be a lifeline for me. He agreed.

I felt exhilarated and full of life. My life was a movie coming to life. I was sure my dad would relent after our marriage and accept us since my happiness was important to him. I actually felt safe again.

I Am Married

I was looking forward to July 3. I was sad that I would have to leave my family behind. We planned to go to the outskirts of town to live at Andy's friend's home for a few days. No one could find us there. Meanwhile, Andy would handle the formalities of getting married in court.

On the 3rd, I planned to leave home at around 1 pm. My parents would be at work. I was thinking that they would eventually be convinced of my decision and see that I really loved Andy. That they would accept him for my sake and everything would end happily, just like in most romantic movies. Never did it cross my mind that this one step of my life would change my entire destiny and lead me to unimaginable paths and experiences.

My parents were a loving couple. They loved each other and the others in the family. They put family first and were always helpful when it came to family and friends. I thought I had found the love of my life, my true partner, my best friend forever, just like Mom and Dad had found each other. Though they were different from Andy and me, I was fixated on the concept of love. And this was the trigger that set me off to do things I normally would not have done. In my dad's words, it would have been unthinkable or unconscionable for me to have thought that I would be taking this step. But here I was, sort of on the brink of madness and ready to do anything for someone who was still a stranger. But see, therein lay a curious fact: I felt safe and happy!

I vividly remember the dress I slipped on after taking a shower on the 3rd of July. A pale brown dress with tiny white and brown flowers. It felt cold on my trembling body. I was constantly thinking of what I was about to do. The trepidation I felt was horrifying, while waves of nausea sent me into a burst of nervous activity. All the time, at the back of my mind, I was thinking of the trail of fire that would follow in a few hours when my parents found out I had run away from home. I knew my father's rage; I had seen it whenever he was confronting injustice being meted out to somebody. I feared his wrath now more than ever. My beloved father, whom I loved and respected. He had never raised his hand or his voice at me. After all, I had been his beloved 'Baby' all this while, his pride. Excellent in studies and sports and 'well-behaved,' as girls of such families are expected to be. I had been a good daughter who did all the right things.

Was this 'good' daughter really, really going to do this? I asked myself. And this overpowering sensation of love — or some other passion, I am not sure — took over. It was intoxicating! I could not focus on anything else. Andy was a strong potion I had drunk. I felt I could never recover from its effects, an inexorable feeling that made me lose all reason. I felt powerless to fight this feeling. It had consumed me completely.

I wrote a letter to my parents that I was going away to get married to the love of my life, whom they did not accept, although he had come and asked them for my hand in marriage. I told them I loved them and respected them but wanted to be married to Andy. I wrote that I would be married by the time they read this letter and that I was safe. I would continue to study and make them proud. I dated the letter and signed it. My hands were trembling when I placed it and my gold necklaces in the grey almirah, knowing I was standing at the point of no return.

It was my mother's routine to change her jewelry every day — almost like a ritual. And when she returned from school in the evening, she would remove her jewelry and put it in a lockbox in the closet. That is when she would find my letter and jewelry that day.

I left home with the dress and sandals I was wearing. I took my birth certificate. This was stuffed into a small 20-inch cross-body bag. I walked out of the home without telling anyone. I shut the door behind me and never looked back. Nor did I think twice.

My mind was in turmoil. I was disrespecting my parents. My dad would be deeply disappointed. Was I doing the right thing? Why did I feel I wasn't doing the right thing? Weren't love and marriage honorable? I thought of all the books I had avidly read. I was troubled, with no friends and no family, and already felt lonely and confused.

I met Andy at Nandita, our regular haunt. I had taken a bus to get there. From there, we left on his motorbike to the outskirts of the city, where his friend lived.

Andy had told his parents he was staying there with me. He told me that our marriage would take place at the Arya Samaj family court and that his family would be attending the ceremony. At that moment, it hit me like a ton of bricks that I had never met his father, his two brothers, and his sister! I had only met his mom. I was stressed, but he assured me that his dad and siblings would accept us.

I felt agitated and wondered for a moment if it was better to go back home and ask my father for forgiveness. At the same time, I felt a strong desire to marry Andy and continue down the path I had chosen. I feared my dad's anger and wasn't sure I could face it. Oh, how conflicted I felt!

In the end, I stayed back. I remember the jeans and white T-shirt that Andy bought for me. I wore it when we went to get our marriage registered at the Arya Samaj court on July 6. The court registrar gave us instructions on how to dress properly for the wedding ceremony that was to take place the next day.

Andy's friend informed Andy's family that the wedding ceremony was at 10 am the next day, July 7. On July 6, he purchased a saree for me. Since I did not have a blouse, I merely hiked up my white shirt to convert it into a makeshift blouse for the red-and-white cotton saree. The person at the court had been particular that I wear a red-and-white saree for my wedding. The red-flowered border with the white background was pretty. I had attended several weddings where the brides wore beautiful white or red sarees and had beautiful hairdos and makeup. There was much fanfare.

My wedding didn't have any of those, but my heart was singing, and that was all that mattered. I could not care less about the gaiety, the ceremonies, or the relatives. There was no gold ring; there was no gold mangal sutra, the typical necklace that an Indian groom ties around the neck of the bride during the wedding ceremony. Andy bought me a fake mangal sutra off the streets of Charminar. When I saw it was fake, I was confused but didn't care.

I wore the saree over my blue jeans, and we went to the Arya Samaj on the morning of July 7. I had none of my family or friends accompanying me. Andy had invited a few of his friends, who attended. Everything was like a dream; I felt it wasn't happening to me but to someone else, and I was watching it from a distance.

I did not understand much of the wedding ceremony, since it took place according to the Hindu custom. I was confused by many of the rituals. Andy and I had to pour oil into the sacred fire with a spoon several times, and each time, the Pundit said, 'Swaha.' I didn't know what the word meant at that time. But that was our cue to take a spoonful of oil and pour it into the fire. We drew the oil out of a quaint-looking vessel. That was the only thing I understood about that ceremony because I had seen it in the movies, and it was the rite of walking around the sacred fire seven times. Apparently, this is the high point of a Hindu wedding.

Andy and I were officially married.

We went back to Andy's friend's home as a married couple, and Andy's family left. I did not feel any different; I was a little tense and tired, although completely happy and thrilled. I forgot about my parents and lived in that moment, which was mine and mine alone. I was joyously married! I slipped back into my jeans and white shirt. We planned to go out for dinner that day. Eleven of Andy's friends attended our wedding and, after the function, accompanied us to his friend's home. This would be our hideout until my dad's anger died down and the coast was clear for me to start living with Andy and his family at their home in the town of Tarnaka.

Dr. Sharon Joshua John

Confusion On My Wedding Night

I was by no means a typical bride — no flowers, no music, no haldi, no henna, and no bridal fanfare. My mind was riding a roller-coaster — sad, happy, confused, sad, thrilled, and angry — mainly because my parents were not by my side. For some strange reason, I had imagined I would be wearing a white dress from one of the finest stores in Paris at my wedding. I wasn't even sure if this was just a dream and if I would soon wake up to my shocking reality on a sweltering July afternoon.

As a child, I always wondered why a bride cried when she left her parents' home. Isn't she supposed to be thrilled to be with the love of her life? I told myself this was a feeling that would soon pass; my parents would be happy, and we would have a grand welcome at home, followed by a reception.

Happy for my husband, who seemed to be thrilled, I suddenly glanced at him and realized that I did not know much about him. Even now, he was nothing more than a stranger to me. I told myself I had an entire lifetime in which to learn more about him. Until death do us part, right? The logical part of my mind tried to drill some sense into me, but my romantic side always got the better of it. Sigh! I have always been a romantic.

Off we went to Blue Diamond, a fancy restaurant back then in Hyderabad, for dinner on our wedding day. I had a marvelous time feasting with Andy and a few of his friends. As the evening passed, I was a wee bit perturbed. Andy had been drinking a lot. The fact was, my dad never drank or smoked and Andy's drinking troubled me a bit. I told myself he was drinking because he was happy. Then why should I be worried? Everyone was happy since we had made it thus far without my dad interfering. Andy's family was very accommodating — or so I thought. I assumed that they were happy, too.

I wished someone from my family or a friend had attended my wedding, but I let it slide. My heart stopped whenever I saw Andy, and the pain and sadness of missing my family vanished. Love brings a tired heart a lot of relief, I must say. My heart would sing again, and all would be well. When I look back now, I don't know whether I was really happy back then or whether I had *imagined* that I was happy. I wonder if, in a sense, the concept of happiness was thrust upon me. Was I trying too hard to be happy? Or maybe, to some extent, it was also because I was in love with the *idea* of love, whether or not I was truly in love with Andy. I probably got carried away by how I thought he was making me feel. Maybe I built a mental image of him and I being in love and was in love with that image.

Again, it occurred to me that I barely knew Andy. I did not know his favorite color, his favorite food, his likes and dislikes, and the little things that made him happy. I discovered that night that he drank a lot. I had known that he smoked but not that he drank so much. Social drinking was acceptable, but drinking excessively was something I did not like. I did not know anything about his family other than that he had two brothers, a sister, and his parents. What did they do? What were they like? No idea. These thoughts were swirling in my head; I felt bewildered at myself.

The next evening, Andy started drinking with his friends again. I did not understand this and felt a little nervous and afraid. I told him, 'I want to go home. I will talk to my dad. He's a good man; he will forgive me. Let me go home.'

Andy grabbed my arms roughly and said in a hoarse voice, his words slightly slurred, 'No! You cannot go. We are married, you're my wife.'

Trying to free myself from his grip, I wept, 'I don't know, Andy, this does not feel right. Maybe I should go.' I cried mainly because everything seemed strange and new to me. I was treading in unfamiliar territory and was extremely agitated about everything. One of Andy's friends' mother was there. She consoled me and counseled me, saying I was married and that this wasn't child's play. I couldn't change my mind on a whim. I should have thought of all this before I left my parents' place. Now my place was with my husband.

I began to learn things about my husband. He drank excessively daily and seemed happier in the evenings. He was a volatile person — lovable one instant and angry or grumpy the very next. He had bouts of foul temper. And yet, he could forgive easily.

He seemed to have a complicated personality. I had to dissect it deeply to know him. I thought his drinking would reduce soon. I was positive I could change him for the better. Maybe this was the Stockholm Syndrome in action. I do not know if this syndrome really exists or not, but I do believe that marriages are made in heaven. That thought made me stay on with Andy. More importantly, I felt safe and protected with him. This was something I hadn't felt in a long, long time — not after my Nainamma had passed away.

Andy's friend's home became our temporary home. I generally woke up at a certain time every morning and studied. I wanted to be a doctor. I was now a wife and made decisions that would not have been comprehensible in my earlier structured life. I wanted to be like my father, who was strong and happy with what he did, working in strange, far-off lands. I also wanted to be like my mother, beautiful and genteel. As children, my brother and I traveled all over the country with my parents, who had taught us that travel was a great way to educate ourselves and learn the ways of the world.

But here, in this temporary home in the days after my wedding, a strange indifference towards my career ambitions set in — a feeling of being carefree and happy, of floating. My situation was deliriously exciting in a curious way, not knowing what the next step in life would be. A month passed in this way. At the end of it, I was weary of being in this temporary home. I was weary of being in limbo.

Meeting my Parents

After a month of marital bliss, it was time for Andy to get back to work. He had missed several days of work. I was weary of staying in this house. I said to him, 'Let's go to your home. I don't think we should stay here any longer. We have availed ourselves of your friend's hospitality for too long already. It's time we went to my place and tried to convince my parents. All will end well.'

Andy's daily excessive drinking troubled me. During the day, he was a different man, pleasant and sensible. At night, he became someone else. I began to feel afraid of him at night. He replied, 'We are married, and this is our honeymoon.'

'Well,' I said, 'It's probably a honeymoon for you because you drink with your friends, but it's not so for me! When you drink, you become an entirely different person.'

He didn't take me seriously and instead said, 'Babe, you're just too cute. You worry about everything. This is not a big issue; I don't drink daily.'

'Yes, you do,' I insisted; he simply ignored me when I brought up his excessive drinking. I thought if we lived in his house in Tarnaka, being with his family would prevent him from drinking so much. Being surrounded by his friends daily was proving to be unhealthy for us.

I was ready to stop this carefree life. Whiling away time was not for me. My honeymoon was over; it was time to put my feet back on the ground, get back to college, and resume studying. I missed my books, I missed my reading, I missed my routine, and most of all, I missed my parents and my brother. I was slowly getting to know my husband better and felt more comfortable around him. He was no more a stranger. I was yet to realize that it takes a lifetime to know someone, and even then, you often just scratch the surface.

At last, Andy agreed to shift back to his home in Tarnaka. We were grateful to Andy's friend and his mom, who had allowed us to stay there for so long. We bid goodbye to them and left for Tarnaka. I was joyful because I could resume my structured life.

We arrived in Tarnaka that afternoon. Again, it hit me that there I was, a new bride who was entering her husband's home with no fanfare or bridal welcome. I consoled myself, saying mine had not been an ordinary wedding; I could not expect much except to be with the love of my life. I had seen several of my friends in college be married off to strangers and lead loveless lives. I thought that was strange and sad and wanted none of that! So, even without the wedding festivities, I was content.

To my dismay, my parents-in-law did not seem too pleased to see me. Apparently, my dad had come to their home almost every day during my absence, furious each time. He wanted me back and yelled and screamed, standing at their gate on the street corner. I was told that the neighbors had watched this daily spectacle. My in-laws could not do anything; we had been unreachable over the phone, and they didn't know our temporary address.

When I heard this, I was mortified. I felt betrayed by my dad. I told Andy, 'My dad is very protective of me. I miss him. I must meet him. We are one family now, let's go and meet my parents and try to resolve the situation.' By that time, all the joy of arriving at my new home had evaporated.

Everything had been sullied by the shocking news about my dad.

My father-in-law was angry with Andy, while my mother-in-law could not understand why my father was not accepting of our marriage. I cried for a little while, feeling like a stranger on my first day in my husband's home.

Evening came. Andy began drinking again. I became increasingly upset, and we had a fight again. Later, he consoled me, and we retired for the night. I dropped into a dreamless slumber, wondering what my life would be like. As we fought that day, I realized that I was in a relationship with a stranger. Try as I might, I could not understand him fully and correctly. I felt I did not understand myself! I felt lost, and I consoled and motivated myself, saying better times were around the corner. I would resume studying soon, and things would be better. I told myself that a rocky start always ended in a beautiful way.

And so began my life in Tarnaka, Hyderabad, in August of that year.

Early the next evening, my dad showed up again. It had become his routine to come there and demand that his daughter be given back by this so-called thug, Andy. This time, he rushed in, wildly flinging the gate open after seeing Andy's motorbike parked in the compound. All of a sudden, I heard a commotion. I rushed out to find my dad, accompanied by a relative. I was overjoyed and frightened at the same time and hid behind Andy as my dad rushed into the house without any fear. When he saw me, he immediately calmed down and asked if we could talk. Andy said, 'Yes, uncle. Please come inside. We are married now.' I could not speak for a while. I stood there simply staring at my dad. He seemed to have lost weight and did not look well. His eyes were sunken, probably from not sleeping enough. I could not help but fall at his feet. 'Dad, please don't be angry with me. I really love Andy. Please forgive me.' I remembered how I had missed him that entire month and felt at peace seeing him.

Dad said, 'Baby, you have to come home. Mummy is very sick. We were very worried about you. Come home, and we will get you married properly in a church. Why are you doing this to all of us?' My heart broke, and I was ready to go back. I looked at my husband and pleaded, 'Andy, let me go home. I shall see my mom and be back soon.'

Andy's reaction shocked me. He was angry. 'Why? *This* is your home now. You have left your parents' home. You seem to have forgotten that you have married me.'

And there it was again, another argument. I consoled my dad, saying, 'We will come in the morning. Don't worry too much.' He didn't seem pleased but left nevertheless. All this while, he asked me a thousand times if I was okay, if I had been harmed, and if anyone had done anything to me. My head was spinning from all this drama. I thought I had lost my mind. I had never gone against my parents before, ever. In fact, it felt natural to be a 'good' daughter.

I, too, was unhappy with the way things had panned out. Everything was difficult and different, and I immediately felt that my free spirit was being restrained. It made me sad to see my dad distraught; I had never before seen him look so pained and sad.

My dad was a wonderful father, husband, and brother, and later, grandfather, too. He came from a family of seven children: four brothers and three sisters. He was the darling of his dad and mom. I guess that is why my Nainamma bestowed a lot of love, blessings, and prayers on me, I being her eldest grandchild. My dad loved me fiercely and was extremely possessive about me. Until he passed away in 2016, he thought the world of me and was very proud of me.

Unfortunately, Andy and my dad disliked each other and fought for several years. How I wish this had not happened! Both of them had complicated personalities. Each was vying for my full attention and was willing to do what they wanted. I, being a fighter, took a different path and set my own course in life.

The next day, Andy and I did not go to meet my parents. My dad came back that evening, demanding that I go back home with him. By then, Andy and his family were enraged. They did not let me go. There was no peace in the household. I decided to stay home until things quieted down. And so, a few more days passed.

My Bachelor's Degree

That summer, life took a strange turn. I lost my routine but went with the flow. I felt a bit wistful, thinking of my dear parents and how they would bestow me with the best of clothing, food, and shelter and pretty much allow me to do as I please. *Those days were over*, I told myself. A new chapter had begun in my life.

I finally received the wonderful news that I had graduated with flying colors. The results of the final exam were announced in the newspaper. Knowing that I had completed my Bachelor's in Science lifted my spirits no end. It was the one ray of sunshine in a gloomy sky. I was excited. Andy and I went to my college, Kasturba Gandhi College, Maredpally, to collect my degree certificate. It was a bright sunny afternoon, and my heart sang as I was planning to resume studying as soon as possible. My dream of having a vibrant career came alive again.

I wasn't sure if my dad was stalking us that day, too. That seemed like his only job. And sure enough, as we were coming out of the college, he jumped at us. Andy's motorbike skidded, and we both ended up on the ground. My dad was dragging me, trying to take me with him. I could not understand what was happening! Everything was a blur. The fall gave me a gash on my knees. I got up, crying. I held on to my dad and said, 'Dad, don't do this, please. I came to get my results from the college.' I was yelling and screaming. The commotion created a big spectacle and brought the cops in a few minutes. All the time, my dad kept telling the cops that I wasn't married and that 'this person,' meaning Andy, had taken his daughter away. I was mortified that the entire college was watching us.

The three of us were taken to the nearest police station. I am not sure how the cops came. Did an onlooker call them? Anyway, the circle inspector questioned all of us. Neither Andy nor my dad could be quietened down. I kept crying intermittently. The inspector asked me who I was and how these two people were related to me. I told him our story briefly, adding that I had been married since July. They let us go. Andy was mad at my dad. His motorbike was partially damaged. Reaching home, he began swearing. Both of us were injured and angry about everything. Andy started drinking, and then, the rest of the day and the whole night went down in tears and pain and arguments with his family.

I loved Andy. His complicated, volatile nature was certainly alarming, yet it seemed to have a strange effect on me. Even at this stage in my life, I am not able to understand what I felt for him or to explain my feelings, thoughts, and decisions from that time.

Andy drank excessively every day. He worked in a nearby town. Most days, he came back home rather late in the night and started drinking. Most of the time, therefore, I was left alone with myself and my thoughts.

Within a few months of getting married, I was in for another rude shock. Andy started bringing several friends home every day and drinking with them until the wee hours of the morning! Yet, he had amazing energy and almost never missed a day at work. Often, I went sleepless — at times, for two days in a row — and made up for it by sleeping the next day after he was gone.

I remember thinking that if he had not drunk so much, he would have been a good person. He did have a good heart and helped many of his friends in times of trouble. I could not understand his complex nature. I think he, too, was tired of the almost daily quarreling with my dad, who still wanted me back. My dad was relentless and created a commotion in front of Andy's house every evening. Sometimes, he would come with a relative. Sometimes, he would be waiting at the corner of the street. On many occasions, he tried to snatch me from the running motorbike! Andy and I often went through dangerous maneuvers, trying to flee from my dad. It was bizarre! I think Andy and Dad, too, went mad during that phase; I wasn't sure of anything anymore.

Thinking of it now, it all seems surreal. I believe the three of us were on different planes in life, each with their own thoughts and battles, trying to figure out how drastically life had changed in the past few months. My dad was a desperate father who wanted his daughter back at any cost. Andy and I realized we had gotten into a marriage too soon, but both of us were too headstrong to admit this to each other and were determined to make it work.

By now, I was quite set in my thinking. This was my home with my husband. I felt safe with him, in spite of the problems I had with his drinking and the daily fights with him and his family. This home was like a haven for me. This was so strange, and I was sad and happy at the same time. I started thinking that I, too, was a complicated creature who probably thrived amidst chaos. Until then, I had had no idea what misery was. Maybe this sudden encounter with misery was something that simply grew upon me. I don't know what exactly the matter was with me back then, but I am sure of one thing: I *thought* I was in love, but this love caused me a lot of pain. Often, people in abusive relationships cope with abuse and tell themselves that *they* have done something wrong, and so deserve the pain. Blaming themselves, though they may not actually be at fault. I did the same, too. I was perplexed at the unbelievable changes I had made in my life, which were completely out of my character.

Andy seemed tired of the fact that my dad was still trying to get me to go back home. My dad became noisier by the day; the street fights were exhausting and extremely embarrassing. I was continuously stressed by the turmoil.

Then, all of a sudden, there was peace. After a few months, my dad stopped visiting and causing a scene at the street corner. Instead, a relative came home to convey the message that my parents had accepted our marriage and had invited us home. I was overjoyed! I could now lead a normal life like other married folks and visit my parents. How sure I was of this! How naïve indeed!

Andy said he did not want to come to my parents' home. After all the trouble my dad had created, he could not believe that things could be normal again. I convinced him that we should meet my parents and it was very stressful for us to continue like this. I wanted to get my books and the rest of my certificates since I needed to begin studying again. Andy unwillingly agreed but said he would drop me at my parents' home and come back later. He did not want to spend time there. He said, 'I will come again in the evening and pick you up.' I agreed.

We visited my parents' house the next morning. I was delighted that this was a time of forgiveness and that things would be normal again. I was nervous since I hadn't seen Mom for almost four months. I kept wondering how my mom and dad would receive me. What about my brother and the other family members? I was filled with trepidation. I was tense and happy at the same time. How was I to know that my life would be like that — abnormally normal — for the next few decades?

Andy stayed at my parents' home for a few minutes. Sensing that nothing untoward would happen to his wife, he left. My mom did not come outside to see him. I went inside, fell at her feet, and asked her to forgive me. She was happy to see me. She hugged me, and everything seemed normal. My other relatives viewed me rather suspiciously but did not say anything, not that I cared for them anyway; the feeling was mutual.

An hour later, my parents said, 'Let's go and see your aunt.' I was happy to see my aunt and uncle and their little children. An hour after we reached my aunt's place, my parents left, leaving me there. My aunt's place was a good two hours from Tarnaka.

It struck me only after they left that I was a prisoner there. My aunt hid my slippers and refused to let me out of her sight. She said that my dad had asked her to keep me there until he came back. I started crying. I was held captive there for three days at a stretch. The door was always locked, and I could not go outside. I said I wanted to go back to my husband's home. I did not have money or any means of transportation.

By the fourth day, I was desperate. I noticed that the house help came there to work early every morning when my uncle and aunt were still in bed. That morning, I waited until she entered the house and slipped out. I walked all the way to Tarnaka. It took me a good four hours. I am not sure how I did it. The blazing sun had my head pulsing and throbbing. This was the second time I was leaving, this time barefoot, with no money or any personal belongings.

I reached Tarnaka in the afternoon, famished and exhausted. The physical pain did not matter much to me. I was euphoric! I walked in through the backdoor. Andy was at home with his mom and brother. I was overjoyed to see him. Both of us held each other and cried. I told him that I never wanted to go back to my parents' home and that I was sorry for being a bad wife. Andy said between tears, 'I missed you a lot. I went to your dad's home, but he told me that you had gone away. I was beside myself with grief. I even went to your other relatives' homes but could not find you.' I was relieved to hear that he had searched high and low for me!

I took a shower and rested with a joyful heart. I felt rejuvenated. Andy and I sat together for a long time. He did not go out that night or drink. I felt betrayed by my parents and was angrier than ever at them for their behavior in trying to imprison me in my aunt's home.

The hurt and pain of losing my Nainamma and moving into my maternal grandma's home, and the memories of living in that joint family, with all its restrictions and the feeling of being unsafe, came back to me and made me very agitated. I could not share these thoughts with Andy; I held my silence. I made up my mind that I would never leave Andy, stay with him, and make my marriage work in spite of the turbulent relationship we had. In those five months since our wedding, I realized that we were poles apart in our levels of ambition, in how we valued education, and in other likes and dislikes. Still, we were similar in ways that I did not yet understand. This similarity was perhaps what kept us together. Both of us were seeking to make our own little world. We were wild and eccentric in our own ways. For the time being, all I felt was relief, joy, and gratitude that I had escaped from my aunt's house and come back to my husband. I felt this experience had made me stronger, and I would now be able to focus on getting ahead in life.

The Violator

I must pause the narration of my married life and rewind to talk about something that deeply scarred me for a long, long time.

I was traumatized when I was 13. This continued well into my late teens. I was frustrated and angry with my parents for not protecting me in spite of knowing about the abuse.

The abuser was a family member. In the beginning, I did not understand the inappropriate touching that took place when I was asleep. But after some time, I began to understand it. I wasn't a typical Indian girl, unlike many of the other young girls who never told anyone about such abuse until late in life. I couldn't be silent and suffer. I told my parents what was happening and named the violator. This was after my Nainamma had died; if she had been alive, this would not have happened. She was my protector in more than one way, other than being my mentor and chief influencer.

India is arguably the largest country in the world, with a joint family system. With space being limited, children in such families are bundled with adults in the same room. In many such families, girls growing into young women face oppression in their own homes, where they are *actually* supposed to feel safe! What a shame! The elders in the family, who are supposed to protect these girls and nurture them, are the very ones who violate them. And the other adults in the family, even if they know what's going on, do not stop the violator from their abominable behavior. Through omission or commission, they let the perpetrators carry on! Worse, they gaslight the girls being abused and make them feel responsible for what's happening to her! The girls grow into women and live in shame, guilt, and misery and are scarred for the rest of their lives.

My mom and Dad did not do much to stop the abuse; it continued even after I told them. I'm not sure what went on behind my back — whether they reprimanded the violator or not — but I felt they should have done more. I was angry most of the time and told myself that I would be my own warrior and advocate; it was my responsibility to protect myself. Who better than I, could do this? I turned to studying harder late into the night and barely slept.

Most nights, I lay in bed half-asleep and tried hard to stay awake, my books strewn around me. The violator was rather bold and touched me inappropriately when the others were sleeping. I would wake up almost instantly, screaming and hitting him, but he was unafraid. He continued his unseemly and uncouth behavior for years until I was well into my teens. A coward — that is what I called him. 'Attack when I am awake, not when I am asleep,' I told him over and over again. I sometimes felt sick and exhausted from protecting myself. When my dad was at home, he would console me and counsel the violator. My mom did not say much. Being meek, she did not know how to handle the situation. But she generally did her best for me in her own way. Or so I think.

I sometimes wonder why my parents did not stop the violator in his tracks immediately. Or why they didn't send me off to boarding school. But who knows? Those times were different. I am sure they did what they could for me. I know they could have and should have done better for their daughter when they knew she was being abused under the same roof!

I look back in time and wonder if *I,* too, could have done something else to make this go away, but I think I did my best under the circumstances. I did whatever I could. Perhaps I should have told my aunts; I am not sure. I did tell one of my aunts, though, years later. She seemed disappointed that I did not tell her when I was being abused. India is certainly not equipped for girls to speak up, though things seem to be changing for the better now. I sure hope so. I think I did my best by telling my parents a child cannot do more than that. Perhaps they did not know how to handle the situation. Counseling the violator was a weak and ineffective move on their part.

Staying awake at night, kicking, screaming, and pushing the violator away was my coping mechanism. And studying until the wee hours of the morning, until sleep overpowered me. Those years of trauma did change me in certain ways. I've no idea what is normal anymore. I console myself, saying things could have been worse and that I did show spirit in fighting back even when I didn't get the support of my parents.

I now understand why I felt safe when I got married to Andy. Why I was able to sleep without fear. I was finally able to banish the horrors of the night from my mind and sleep peacefully. This was so liberating! No wonder, too, that I thought this was love — maybe it really was, but it was complicated love, for sure! In spite of its madness, there was peace and a sense of calm in it. It was fascinating to see that Andy, in spite of his violent behavior, was the type of person who could kill someone for me. He was the sort of person who can come into your life only once.

Strangely, when I visited my parents' home after marriage, the violator never approached me at any time. The sensation of being protected washed over me all over again. Andy was my guardian angel. This feeling seemed to be heavier than anything else. And so, after that debacle of being caged in my aunt's home by my parents, I decided that my life in my parents' home was over. I was now a wife and was determined to live my life with Andy and make the best of it.

After getting married, I managed to block out thoughts of the violator. But the awful memories came back to haunt me 19 years later after Andy died. The lonely bed brought back all sorts of bad memories. I was fearful to sleep. All this after 19 strange and tumultuous years with Andy. In all the years I was with him, I never shared this part of my life with him. I knew how he would have reacted. The kind of person he was, mercurial and possessive- made him difficult to understand, he would have certainly murdered the violator.

When Andy died, I felt as if my protective shield had been ripped off. I was left fragile yet strangely strong enough to cope without him. Andy left me with two little children. He drank himself to death. I felt guilty that I could not change him with my love or my professional success. All the counseling, the advice to join AA, the trips to rehab, the constant begging and pleading fell on deaf ears. He wouldn't listen to me or anyone else. Andy would not quit drinking. He felt he could not! At times, I feel really betrayed by him.

My parents visited me within a month after Andy died. I was in New Orleans in the United States of America then. I confronted them and asked them why they had not done anything to the violator even when I had complained to them. My parents tried to look away as I asked them, 'Was counseling him enough? Don't you think you could have done something more?' It was the first time I was confronting them about this matter. Probably, living in the States had made me bold enough to do so.

Both of them sat in stony silence. My dad lowered his eyes, and my mom's face was expressionless. Their silence made me think that they had not thought that the continued abuse would have such a great impact on me. Or, perhaps they thought I was strong enough to fight back like a wild girl and I did not need their protection. I don't know. I stopped being sure of anything a long time ago.

The fear of sleeping in that house in Hyderabad haunted me for a long time. I read a lot about sexual abuse in India and how it impacts the minds of a young person. My life would have been different if my dad had stormed out of the room and charged at the violator. How ironic that it was finally the wild and violent Andy who made me feel protected. I can empathize with those who are raped or are abused in other ways by family members; *I know how they feel*. My traumatic experience made me angry and feel abnormal. It triggered a multitude of emotions in me. Many women stay silent out of shame, fear, and unnecessary guilt. They blame themselves. They do not speak up about the abuse or the abuser; they take the trauma to their graves.

But I wasn't silent; I argued with myself. I did not keep quiet. I fought back. I am proud of this. I often ponder over the things that shaped me into what I have become. My parents were wonderful, kind-hearted people who constantly sought opportunities to transform evil into good. I don't hold anything against them. They loved me truly, and I, too, loved them with all my heart. They gave me the best of everything. Being a parent myself, I know that all parents want the best for their children. They want them to excel in everything.

But parents have their weaknesses, too. As a parent myself, I know that parents are not perfect.

I credit myself for not losing my sanity and holding on to my goal of getting ahead in life. Growing into my teens, I was filled with rage. The violator kept me in that state most of the time. Strangely, in the days when he was abusing me, I wasn't afraid of *him*. I was afraid of sleep. Because that was when I would be at my weakest and lowest moment, I could not protect myself when I slept. Before I lay on my bed, I would whisper to myself, *don't sleep, don't sleep.* I hated myself when I had to give in to deep sleep on some occasions and couldn't stay alert.

In time, I have learned to forgive the violator. This is what I have learned from my dad and my Nainamma; they instilled in me the belief that the most important trait a human can have is the ability to freely forgive when people change. They taught me the power of forgiveness.

More importantly, I rose above my anger and became firmer in my resolve to excel in life. I thank God that, because of the fear of sleep, I was able to put those sleepless nights to good use — by studying to get a bright future and leave home.

When I confronted my parents in New Orleans about my abuse, I felt better for getting it off my chest. I keep thinking that I left my past behind a long time ago, but one can never really leave one's past completely behind, can they? I was safe in America years and years later, but the price I paid for my safety was way too high.

Dr. Sharon Joshua John

My First Child

I was pregnant! It was a joyous occasion for me. The very feeling of a baby growing within me was exhilarating! A mother - I was going to be a mother soon. The awful morning sickness did not allow me to venture outside to study or work. I did not want my child to have a difficult life. Now that I was married and pregnant, my dream of becoming a doctor was fast fading. I was forced to think of another path to reach my dream country, the USA.

I was relegated to being a typical housewife: waking up in the morning, fixing breakfast, and helping my mother-in-law tend to the household chores. I hated every second of my life during that time — not knowing the future and loathing myself for that. I wanted to be a mother, but I also wanted to go back to college. I didn't want to sacrifice my dreams of a vibrant career at the altar of motherhood. Never in my life had I planned to lead the life of a typical housewife. I was a bird who wanted to spread her wings wide and explore the infinite sky. The whole world awaited me; my career and a bright future called to me. And yet, here I was, washing dishes in a dingy home. *Would I be chained to this life forever? Have I destroyed my life? Is there no way out of this chained situation?* These questions hammered away in my head all the time, making me feel claustrophobic and nauseated.

And to add further worries to my woes, my dad, even now, was relentless in his attempt to break up my marriage. Unbelievable! I failed to understand him. My relationship with him was complicated. *Most things* in my life were, and have been, complicated! I loved him as deeply as my father but did not wish to listen to his 'words of wisdom.' I was set in my ways of thinking and wanted to choose my own path in life. In that sense, I was my father's daughter and still am.

I was in the midst of strife and hatred. Fights with Andy and his family were a daily routine. Andy's brother, too, drank excessively, resulting in arguments and fights between the brothers, often leading to bloodshed. The brothers did not seem to be at peace without a fistfight. I was shocked at this behavior; I had never seen my parents fight or argue like this. And yet, for all the mess, life here seemed better than in my own dysfunctional joint family, which was full of dark, forbidden secrets — skeletons in the cupboard.

In January of the first year of my marriage, Andy and his parents decided to throw a wedding reception, though it was, by then, almost six months since our wedding. Andy's relatives and several people in our community did not know we were married. In India, it is customary to invite the entire community for a post-wedding reception that includes dinner. Several arguments ensued about financing the dinner. Of course, I had no money to contribute. Andy's parents knew they could not approach my parents for obvious reasons. Finally, Andy took a loan from his pension contribution and was able to host the dinner.

I was thrilled since I was pregnant and finally got to dress like a bride. I invited three of my friends from college to the dinner. Andy bought me a beautiful yellow-and-red-gold saree. His aunt allowed me to borrow her gold jewelry for the evening. Andy was dressed in a suit; he looked very handsome. My mind was at peace, and I was overjoyed. Amidst a gathering of 50 or so, we had a wonderful time, a time of laughter and happiness, celebrating each other and sharing our love and affection with everyone. We thought we should invite my parents, but after some second thoughts, we decided not to invite anyone from my family.

Alas, the hours of happiness were short-lived. Andy's oldest brother got into a drunken brawl with him as the reception progressed into the night. Soon, the brawl took an ugly turn, and people began to leave, seeing the drinking and the fighting. Andy broke his brother's jaw, and his brother lost two teeth. The screaming wouldn't stop. Andy's brother had to be taken to the hospital. And so, the night ended in something I can never forget. When I was married in the family court, I hadn't been dressed as a typical bride. At the reception, I thought I finally had my moment, but the memory is now tainted forever.

Isn't marriage supposed to bring joy, peace, and love? Well, mine brought none of it. All it brought was strife, pain, and anger. It was awful. I sat down on the steps outside the venue of the reception, my mind roiling at the turn of events.

Andy's mother always took Andy's brother's side, and this made Andy angrier. And so, life went on, normally abnormal.

Over the next few months, I became anxious since my parents did not reconcile with Andy and I. Night chased day, week chased week, and the months passed by. I became morbidly obsessed with the thought that I would remain the housewife that I never wanted to be. The feeling of being trapped in this hellhole for a lifetime resurfaced. I wanted to get out and break free. My undergraduate degree certificate lay safely in my custody, whereas all my other certificates were still with my parents. They kept it with themselves in the hope that I would come back to get them or perhaps that Andy would throw me out of his home, knowing that I came with nothing. I entered my husband's home with nothing and left with two suitcases — to come to America in 1998. In the intervening years, I equipped myself with the wealth of knowledge — my PhD — that would take me to America.

I thank God for giving me wisdom and helping me through the rest of my 15-odd years or so. My Nainamma taught me well. The teachings of compassion and service have remained an integral part of my life. Nainamma often said, 'Education is the wealth that can never be taken away, the gold that never loses its shine, and the iron that never gets rusted.'

'Treasure it,' she would say before adding, 'It will take you to heights you can never dream of.'

Pregnancy brought a new lease of life and renewed strength with the thought that it was now or never. I needed to start somewhere soon. Within a few months of marriage, I was disillusioned. My rosy dreams of 'happily ever after' were never a thing in my life, and I soon realized that this would not change. I was the man in the relationship, and I needed to pull my little family together.

The child growing within me renewed my spirit with new hope and offered a fresh lease of life. I told Andy I wanted to work; studying seemed to be out of the question just then, but I thought if I could bring in some money, he would allow me to pursue higher studies later. My morning sickness began to recede, and I was much better, both in my spirit and in my body. I began to work as an administrative assistant at a typewriting institute nearby. *Clack, clack, clack:* I hated the sound of the horrible clacking of the keys but had to tolerate it. Every day, I went to the institute at 10 am and returned home at 3 pm. The students came at different times of the day to learn typing and shorthand. When there were no students, I was allowed to practice typing.

I worked there for four months. I could no longer work as, I was heavily pregnant by then, nearing the end of my term.

That institute gave me my first exposure to typing. I initially used one finger to type and was exasperated with myself. I thought *this is too funny*! *What the heck is wrong with me, typing with a single finger ASDFLKJH - clack, clack clack.* Ridiculous! Like playing the piano. I didn't think much of this art of typing. If only one could use this skill to play the piano like Beethoven, sigh! What was I thinking? I could not imagine myself doing something like this for the rest of my life, so I began to think of other ways of studying further and bettering myself.

By now, I was being neglected by Andy. I am not sure if he loved me or if he tried to control my untamed spirit. He, for one thing, hadn't contended that I would be a fighter. I demanded his undivided attention and would not take second place in his life. I constantly fought with him when he started seeing other women, which seemed to be the usual with him.

Heavily pregnant, I often waited for him till 1 am in the morning. Some nights, he never came back home. We seemed to drift apart even before the birth of our first child. Not even a year had passed by, and my marriage was already in shambles. I felt helpless. I wasn't sure if this was love or passion. I did not want to leave him, even though he was seeing other women. I guess it was the sense of safety that kept me with him through all the tumult.

Nothing is more insulting to a woman than the fact that her man prefers another woman to her. But if Andy was a philanderer, I was a fighter and was relentless every time he came back. I would somehow know that he had been with another woman. He became emboldened and began to boast to me about his escapades, which, he said with arrogance, were mere flings as if that made a difference! He would add that, at the end of the day, I was his wife, the woman who was having his child. Why do all womanizers feel that a wife should feel blessed that her husband came back to her? Would a womanizer be as accommodating if his wife returned to him after being intimate with another man? No way! I don't think I could have done anything better at that time than focus on the baby and on my education, which would make a better life. Of course, I hoped Andy would change for the better. I began to make excuses in my mind for his behavior, that he had grown up as a wild child since the age of 14 and had not received proper parental guidance. My relationship with him was like the ebbing of the tides, sometimes high and sometimes low. Sometimes, I felt he loved me and could do anything for me, whereas at other times, I felt he did not care for me at all. All in all, the confusion in my mind did not allow me to think straight. My fate hung in the balance of destiny. I was alone with my thoughts and could not share them with anyone.

My daughter arrived in June of the next year. There she was, the tiniest bundle of joy. For hours, I would stare at her cute little fingers, tiny nose, and sweet lips. She was my peace and solace.

My mother-in-law and sister-in-law were with me the night my daughter was born. Andy arrived in the morning, after work. He did not stay for a long time; he hung around for an hour or so and then left with his friends. 'To celebrate,' he said. I cried when he left so soon. I am not sure if he was ready to be a father. He probably went with the flow. Even after the baby came, he led a carefree life, drinking excessively on a daily basis and hanging out with his friends. This incurred the wrath of his father as well, and they often fought.

The day our daughter was born, Andy received his transfer orders to Hyderabad. I was relieved. For the past several years, he had been trying to get this transfer. This was certainly an auspicious sign, I thought. The birth of our baby girl heralded luck for our family. My daughter was my lucky charm, the carrier of joy and luck.

When he started working in Hyderabad, Andy left home at 5 am and returned in the evening. After that, he went out with his friends. I was amazed by his energy. I was happy that he would be around the baby. I hoped things would improve and that he would stay home in the evening, too.

But that was not to happen. Andy seemed to think that a wife should stay home, take care of the home and the children. I was enraged by his attitude; we often got into arguments that ended in my tears. Then we made up. Until we fought again. If the fights were bitter, the patch-up was extra sweet. It was a constant battle, or dance, of love and hate. Keen to take up a job, I told him I could not continue like this, and perhaps I should try my hand at being a teacher — since that seemed to be the most convenient job for me at this point in time. At least I had my Bachelor's degree in science and could do something with it. I did not want to depend on anyone, including my husband. To me, real freedom comes with financial independence; I have always been fiercely independent. I wanted to earn my living, even if it meant receiving the meager salary of a teacher.

Andy's parents agreed. My mother-in-law was a teacher, too, and it was the best thing I could do with my bachelor's degree at that time. I had to get permission from Andy and his parents for everything, including taking up a job. I had to get their permission to go out of the house. I felt awful and claustrophobic. I hailed from a family of strong women who were great teachers. Following their path, I settled for a teaching career temporarily, assuming that would be the easiest route to take. It would help me make some sort of a beginning. Later, I could think of moving up the career ladder. I felt I would cease to exist or breathe if I did not start working and remained a housewife. *Rise, rise*! I told myself. *Get out of Hyderabad*! But for that, I had to be financially secure; I did not have any money. My daughter needed care, and later, an education. She was a few months old when I started working as a science teacher at a high school nearby.

I took the public bus to school every day. Andy's parents took care of my daughter when I was at work. Returning in the evening, I would take care of our daughter. By nightfall, I was exhausted after taking care of our daughter and helping with the household chores.

Andy's fights with his brothers and father and his drinking continued in the background. One of those days, I learned that Andy had started drinking from the age of 14! But for this, I could not fault him alone. One is a child of one's circumstances, so to speak. Andy was a high school dropout. He was then put to work by his father and spent most of his time from the age of 14 to his late twenties with men who were much older than him. These people were a strong influence on him and probably got him into the drinking habit. After all these years in bad company, it seemed impossible for him to get out of the toxic twosome of bad friends and drinking. They seemed to take priority over me, our daughter, and everything else.

Our neighbor, Mr. Nanda Kumar, often came to break up Andy's fistfights with his brother. The other neighbors merely watched. When it became a street nuisance, the cops would come and break up the fights after issuing a warning, which would never be heeded.

My routine was hectic. My daughter kept me awake most nights; I was working during the day and had to get ready with my lesson plan for the next day; I was beyond exhausted. Somehow, I faced every difficulty with a cheerful heart, knowing this too would soon pass. Since Andy was working in Hyderabad, it was convenient for him. He often came back home late at night and went to work at around eight the next morning after dropping me at the bus stop. Life continued. I had come to a point where I forced myself not to feel any pain but to know that someday I would find the place that could really be called home. It would be suffused with peace, love, and joy.

I took comfort in my daughter, bathing her and dressing her. Every month, I gave my meager salary to Andy on the 1st, the day I got paid. I must admit that he was very hardworking. Since we lived in a joint family, it was a given that Andy and I had to pay for our stay at Andy's parents' house. So, from our salaries, we paid up our share of the stay. The spacious house could accommodate all of us comfortably. I was relieved that I wasn't a burden on anyone and that we had something to get by.

My financial condition was very difficult, but I happily made do with the little I had. I often looked for good deals on the streets on Secunderabad Station Road and bought my daughter clothes and little trinkets at a bargain. She was a living doll. I loved to dress her up. Little things like combing her curly mane, dressing her up in cute little dresses, and applying a black dot on her temple filled me with great joy. I used my mother-in-law's sewing machine to sew clothes for my daughter. Things were slightly different in my daughter's case than it had been in mine. My parents had given me the best of everything in my childhood. They had bought me the best of clothes from the best stores in town. Those days were gone. Strangely, I did not feel sad. I embraced myself simply because I felt great, earning and doing something constructive with my life.

I took great joy in embroidering my daughter's clothes and sometimes took almost a month to embroider her blouses. She was the most beautiful child I had ever seen; she gave me great joy amidst the crisis and the drudgery at home. I still cherish the memories of dressing her up in clothes I had stitched myself.

When I brought home my salary, I rationed out a limited amount of money for things like my bus fare and kept a little pocket money for myself. Beyond this, I had no control over my own salary. This went on even after I moved to the United States. Every rupee and every dollar had to be accounted for. Twenty years ago, I was buying cheap clothing off the dirty and dusty streets of Secunderabad. And here I am now, able to afford clothes from the most expensive stores in the world!

Life has taken its toll on me with its harshness and cruelty, yet it has bestowed upon me much grace and blessings, too. I do not forget the time when I struggled to buy a cup of tea from a small eatery. It was a luxury to have a Bru instant coffee, which is still my favorite. When I feel hopeless at times, I look back into my past and think that this too shall pass.

I shared a violent, complicated relationship with Andy, which swung from passion to love and then to hate and back. This continued until 2003. He, too, shared the same feelings towards me. This was what probably kept us together for so many years. The person who could inflict the most terrible pain on me was also the person who could give me great joy. The fact that we were poles apart made us stick to each other till his last breath. Don't they say that opposites attract? Soon, I stopped being perennially confused. Now, the lines were much clearer. Many a time, clear lines would cross over and become a tangled mess. I accepted this and continued to move forward.

Most people, including my dad, did not understand it. I did not expect them to when I did not understand it myself. People thought I was madly in love or mad to accept this violent relationship. I continued to cope and survive, living life in careful mental compartments. I could make changes to some compartments; to others, I could not. But more importantly, I was independent. It changed my perspective on living and surviving to move ahead in life. The birth of my daughter heralded a new chapter in my life. It stopped my drifting mind and brought me back on track to pursue a higher education and move to America. I realized it was *my life, my story*. I would not allow anybody else to hold the pen and write the story of my life. Only *I* would write it — with determination. And right now, as I am writing down the story of my life for you to read, I can't help thinking all over again that truth is stranger than fiction.

Dr. Sharon Joshua John

The First Beating

Andy never stayed at home during the evenings. He came back home, drunk, at midnight or later. By that time, I was angry and waiting for him, and we often argued till the wee hours of the morning at times.

My daughter was six months old when the violence began. Strangely, I wasn't surprised by it. It was more like, 'Bring it on. I was waiting for it. You can hit me, but I will not back down.'

It all began one night. As usual, he came back late. And as usual, he demanded that I come to bed immediately. I was exhausted and irritated that night. The baby had been crying all evening. I had had a long day at work and had tended to the household chores. He kept asking me to do his bidding, and I kept insisting that I was too tired. He kept dragging me to bed, and I kept repeating, 'No, no, no!' Not used to taking no for an answer, he got up, came up from behind, grabbed my hand, and pulled me backward. Startled, I twisted my hand out of his grip. This enraged him. He immediately struck me from behind and pulled me again, fistfuls of my hair in his hand.

I could not react for a moment. Then I screamed, 'You hit me! You hit me!' and did not stay down. That was my undoing. The blows began to rain on me. I fought back like a wild cat. He was shocked. He kept pounding me. He kicked me in my stomach. Everything became a blur. I had no idea how he got me onto the floor. He demanded an apology. But I said, 'No, no, no, I will not apologize.' I was screaming like a banshee. I had become immune to the physical pain, and all the pent-up frustration and anger was rising in me in tidal waves.

I could not think straight. The baby woke up crying, and my mother-in-law rushed into our bedroom. All hell broke loose. Andy's father, too, joined the fight. My daughter, by now, was screaming her lungs out. Andy was shouting, I was shrieking, there was utter chaos.

Andy grabbed me like a doll and hurled me down the hallway. My head was throbbing as he yanked me. My mother-in-law was screaming at her son. I saw her, this tiny lady about four feet tall, trying to stop her son and me. Somehow, she looked like she was dancing. I spun around and pulled Andy's hair. I, too, was deranged with anger. Finally, I gave up; he was too strong for me. I fell down, convulsing and sobbing. He thought I had given up. Suddenly, I got up, picked up my daughter, and ran out the front door. Andy pulled me back, snatched the baby, and hit me again. I fell down into a pool of my blood.

I did not know what to make of this. Thus began the violence that went on even when I moved to the USA. By that time, my body had taken so many beatings that when he beat me, it felt like nothing. I was unbroken. Even as my body took the terrible beatings, my mind and spirit remained untouched. I soared far, far away into another world, a world without Andy.

As the months went by, I became demanding and paranoid and surrendered to rage. My rage made me stronger. After a night's beating, I would force myself to wake up the next day, though in a daze. Andy asked me one morning, 'Are you okay? Why do you fight me? I love you. Don't fight me; you won't win. You should not have done that last night.

Why can't you be a normal girl, like I thought you were?' I saw something in his eyes. I thought he was going to say sorry and would not beat me again.

He gathered me in his arms, pressed himself to me, and said, 'You don't need to work or study. I will take care of you.' *Really?* I thought cynically. I got out of his embrace and checked myself. Thank God I had no broken bones. I would be okay. He could not touch my mind. He could not take my dreams away; no one could do that.

That year continued in this vein. I wove in and out of happiness and sadness. When Andy beat me, I was sad. When he made up with me, I was happy. My mind tricked my body into thinking that this was nothing, that there was hope ahead and more to life than this. I had the breath of life; with every breath, I could make a change. *This is not the end; this is not the end*, I kept thinking. *This is the beginning, the beginning of something brighter and better*. I told myself that, each day of my life, I would go on till the end, weaving between sadness and happiness. This weaving, in and out, is a normal part of everyone's life.

We lived close to Osmania University. Sometimes, I went to the library on the university campus and read up on all the courses I could take. I was wondering how I could better myself since I saw no hope in depending on Andy and his family. I spent an hour in the library, at least on alternate days, trying to find the cheapest and the fastest way to get ahead academically. Nothing seemed plausible. I was afraid that I wouldn't be able to study further, and no one cared about it. Andy himself did not think it was important for me to study further. Come to think of it, he didn't think it was important for me to study or work. He thought we had enough to put food on the table. I could not understand how a person could be so unambitious and have no goals in life. I thought it was unconscionable to live without goals.

Since I came from a family of teachers and the Bachelor's degree in Education was for a year, I thought I could try my hand at this. I decided to appear for the entrance examination. If I was selected as a merit candidate to be admitted to the University, it would cost me around Rs. 90, which was less than 2 US dollars. If I wasn't selected as a merit candidate, the tuition fee would be much higher, and there was really no way I could pay. I bought books from the second-hand bookstore near Secunderabad railway station to study for the entrance exam. I began to prepare in earnest. The exam was a month away.

I finally found my wandering heart stabilized somewhat. The thought that I was going back to college made me feel powerful. I told Andy and his parents that I wanted to study to become a teacher. They were indifferent about it. Not that what they thought mattered to me. They did not know that my goal was to get a better education and a future in the States. I had officially given up on Hyderabad and was willing to wait and work towards my goal. *Baby steps*, I told myself, *baby steps*. And I began to grow stronger in spirit. And then there was my beautiful daughter, who gave me great comfort and joy. She brought peace and strength to my soul.

Bachelor's Degree in Education

I was accepted into the Bachelor of Education (B.Ed.) program. I was overjoyed! In this program, two years of regular study had been packed into one intense year. There was no way I could continue working as a teacher *and* study. I decided to quit my job. It would be for a year only and would pass in the blink of an eye. Completing my B.Ed. would land me a better job as a teacher at a better salary. Andy seemed to be okay with my decision. His parents were thrilled that I had received a merit-based scholarship and that they would not have to bear the burden of taking care of a daughter-in-law who had come with no dowry. After all, a teaching job with a teaching degree paid well. It was considered a decent career for a mother in those days.

My dad still tried to meet me. He wanted me to come back to live with him and Mom, although I had a baby now. They were concerned about their baby, and I was concerned about mine. I had to meet my parents since I needed all my original school and graduation certificates. I had to submit them to Andhra Mahila Sabha as part of the admission process for my B.Ed. I thought my parents would soften when they found that I was continuing on the academic path and would accept my marriage, at least now.

I sent word to my parents through a relative that I had passed the entrance examination and needed my certificates. My dad arrived the same evening with my certificates. He seemed overjoyed to see the baby but was quite shocked to see my state. I was delighted to see him. I took my certificates, thinking that everything would be fine now, with the moral support of my parents.

Andy's daily excessive drinking wore me down. I often pleaded with him. I said I loved him and that he had to change drinking and hurting me. His drinking was bad for his family, although he didn't realize that. Sometimes, my despondency gave in to depression. I constantly reminded myself that it was like taking a bath every day. I had to bathe with hope daily and plod on, living life in compartments. Strangely, living life in compartments has always been my forte. I could be sad for myself and happy for my daughter. I could ignore Andy's behavior and focus on my daughter and my education. This defense mechanism worked well. I told myself, 'I will survive; things could be worse.'

Three months into my B.Ed., one afternoon, I spotted Andy on his motorbike. I was at the Andhra Mahila Sabha bus stop when he whizzed past me on his bike with a woman riding pillion. Like I said earlier, I knew he was cheating on me with other women, but that was the first time I was *seeing* him with another woman. To see him with a woman who was clinging to him tightly enraged me. I did not wait for the bus but took an autorickshaw home, although it was expensive.

Predictably, Andy wasn't at home. My rage knew no bounds. I fought with my mother-in-law and waited for Andy. He came back well past midnight, fully drunk, as usual. As he was parking his motorbike, I rushed towards him and said, 'Where did you go? I saw you at 5 pm this evening with a woman on your motorbike.' I barraged him with questions. He swatted me like a fly and said, 'None of your business where I go and who sits on my motorbike.'

'Really? Really?' I was incoherent with rage. 'It *is* my business! I am your *wife*! The baby has a cold and fever; she needed to go to the hospital!'

'Yes,' he retorted, 'And you went to college instead of taking care of the baby.'

By that time, it had turned into a free-for-all. I started shouting, and he began hitting me. The blows rained on me. I fell down, tasting dirt in my mouth. I tried to fight back, but it was futile. He was too strong for me. I sat there in the dirt, yelling and screaming, refusing to back down. Andy's father and mother, too, joined the fight. They thought I needed to keep quiet, but I refused to participate in this nonsense. They told me to back down, saying their son was drunk. 'When is he not drunk?' I asked them.

I was fed up by now. I felt like a dog who was licking her wounds. I rose and dusted my saree. My hair was disheveled. I took a shower and changed my clothes. Thankfully, the baby had slept through the ruckus peacefully. *How blissful it is to be a child*, I thought. I wonder what babies think or what dreams they have, if at all. I saw my little angel smile in her sleep and wondered if she spoke to God and the angels. I wished she could convey the message to God that her father needed to change and change immediately. What a strange thought!

Early the next morning, I again demanded an explanation from Andy, and the fight started in the morning itself. Andy's parents were fed up with me; they thought I was like my father, boisterous and unruly. They said I was a street fighter. I could not control my anger.

Andy got dressed and left for work, as usual. That day, I did not help my mother-in-law or go to college. My mind was in turmoil; I did not understand what I should do or say. I busied myself with taking care of the baby and remained in our bedroom most of the time. The others weren't bothered about me. By now, the house was silent. My mother-in-law had left to see a friend in the neighborhood. My father-in-law lived in an outhouse of sorts, entering the main house during mealtime or when he heard a commotion between the brothers. Andy's brothers had also left. I was alone with my baby and my thoughts, smarting from desperation and hopelessness.

I could not take this. I decided to go back to my parents' house. I packed my backpack with the few belongings I had and the baby's things and walked out. I took a bus to my parents' house. Neither my dad nor my mom were at home. The other members of the family looked at me suspiciously. That was the first time they were seeing my daughter; they were happy to see her.

I waited anxiously for my mother. It was now 6 pm. I thought by now Andy's family would have known that I had left with the baby.

When my mom came home and saw me, she was very disturbed. No, she was terrified! She asked me to go back to Andy's house. My dad had gone to Indore, a neighboring state, on a drilling contract, and there was really no one who could fight with Andy. My brother too had gone with my dad. My mom said, 'Baby, when Dad comes back, I will ask him to go and fetch you from Andy's house.' My mom was mortally afraid of Andy.

I argued with her and broke down. I was desperately looking for refuge and was mortified at the thought of having to go back to that hell. Perhaps my daughter sensed my pain and frustration; she started crying, too. I demanded some money from my mother, which she gladly gave. I also asked for Dad's address in Indore, which she gave. I told her I would send him a letter asking him to come back and take me out of this hell I had landed myself in. I was beyond myself by then and had no rational thought. I took my daughter and my backpack and left my parents' house around 6.30 pm. I did not want to be there any longer lest Andy should arrive.

As I stepped out of my parents' house, I made an impulsive decision. I headed to the railway station. I decided I was going to meet my dad in Indore. I was not going back to my husband's home.

I was taking a huge risk. I wasn't sure if and how I would find my dad; he could very well be on the move since he was a driller. I wasn't even sure if I would find him at the address my mother had given me. During our summer holidays when we were kids, my dad would take my brother and me on his drilling trips. They would drill in remote areas, oftentimes in the middle of a forest area. There was no phone or no way to reach him from his base.

I looked at my daughter, that tiny and trusting creature. All I could see were her large eyes gazing at me. *So innocent*, I thought. I bought a ticket and boarded a train to Indore. It would take a good 24 hours to reach that State and city. I was traveling in an unreserved coach. In these coaches, people could take any seat, stand anywhere, or sit on the floor. I plonked myself in a corner of the coach, squatting on the floor with my daughter. I remember thinking, sitting on that grubby floor, that babies are very fortunate. They live on love, fresh air, and milk.

I could find milk for her at stops along the way. I fed her and changed her clothes from time to time. I found it comical to see her so happy, the wind flying off my face. In India, the unreserved train coach is a place where extremely poor people travel. Almost all of them are men; no woman travels in it of her own volition. The coach was packed to the gills and unkempt. One couldn't get to the toilet easily.

I was the only woman in this coach. Several men were looking at me curiously. I did not look like someone who would travel under these conditions. Luckily, seeing my daughter, they seemed rather open to giving me space to sit down in a corner on the floor. I laid my daughter on the floor of the train and swaddled her in a blanket. The wind was terrible, howling through the open doors and windows. I wrapped my saree tightly around myself, covered my head, and dozed off. I could not even cry at that time; I wasn't sure what the future held.

That was the time I desperately needed my dad. Somehow, he always seemed to know what to do and how to encourage me. He always had solutions to my problems. I kept thinking of Andy, and the memories of the gut-wrenching pain he had caused me broke my heart all over again. I was terribly agitated. I thought that I would be missing college, but I felt helpless. Anyway, here I was, spending the night on a train traveling with a little baby. Was I reckless? Mad? I wasn't sure about my actions; all I knew was that I was going to seek my dad for help. I knew he would accept me, no matter what.

We traveled the entire night into the next day. It was such a slow train! It was exhausting to sit on the floor. I could not sleep the entire night. Traveling during the day was safer, and I felt better as we neared Indore. I anxiously read the names of the stations we halted at. I hoped we would reach Indore before nightfall and find my dad quickly. I kept looking at my watch. Another thirty minutes to go; it was almost 7 pm. By the time the train crawled into Indore, it had taken more than 24 hours from the time it left Hyderabad! Thankfully, my daughter had slept peacefully through most of the journey. She must have liked the cool breeze.

How will I find my dad? Where is the place where he lived? Is he even in town? These questions raced through my mind as the train slowed down and stopped at Indore railway station. I felt like Lakshmibai, the queen of Jhansi, fighting her enemies with her kid on her back. I was fighting the demons in my life who were trying to hold me down and drag me to hell. And I had a little baby in my arms.

Unwittingly, my daughter taught me to make the best out of a hopeless situation. I felt safe, holding her close to my chest and stomach. This seemed strange, too, since I was the parent who needed to make *her* feel safe.

I was standing at the door to my coach, my daughter, in a makeshift sling when my heart leaped. There was my dad, standing on the platform, sipping tea with another person! Relief and panic hit me together. I started screaming, 'Daddy! Daddy! Daddy!' Without thinking, I jumped from the moving train to the consternation and utter shock of the onlookers. I gasped as I landed on the platform, nimble on my feet. Oh, joy! The years of jumping up and down the roof of our home and the mango tree had come in handy.

My dad came running. This bizarre sight of me, hundreds of miles away from Hyderabad, seemed to have shaken him. He was speechless and stood frozen. He had this look of utter shock tinged with relief. I ran to him, crying. My dad was the anchor of my sinking life. I hugged him tightly and said between sobs, 'I came here to see you.'

He still could not utter a word. That was the only time in my life when I saw him in such a state. Gathering his wits at last, he fumbled, 'What…what…what exactly is going on here? How is the baby? Is she alright?' He hurriedly took her in his arms.

He then flooded me with questions. 'What happened? How did you come? Where is Andy? And Mummy?'

Unable to hold back my pain, I told him everything that had happened. Since there was no long-distance phone nearby, we immediately went to the post office in the station, and my dad shot off a telegram to Mom, simply writing, 'Baby landed here with Christina. She is safe.' Christina is my daughter's name. I could imagine my mom's shocked reaction when she read the telegram. She would be definitely worried, hurt, and upset at the turn of events. Only her daughter, the wild child, could be unpredictable and behave like this.

My dad said, 'Baby, thank God you are okay. What were you thinking, coming like this and jumping off the moving train holding a baby? Anyway, you are lucky you saw me. I was leaving Indore to go to the drilling site, which is a good two hours away, and would have come back after a few days.' The sheer terror of what I would be doing in a strange place, not knowing anyone, reflected in his eyes and his tone. In those days, India was not a place where one, especially a lone woman with a baby, could take a hotel room just about anywhere. I looked up at my dad and smiled, saying, 'Oh well, I am my father's daughter.'

My dad was happy and thrilled beyond measure to see the two of us. We proceeded to his drilling location. It was such fun! I felt like I was six years old again, riding the drilling rig with Dad. My brother and I had ridden the drilling rig as children; it was massive. We also rode huge trucks with my father. I had always found his job interesting. I had often seen him standing at a borewell, sending the heavy rods into the bore, often working for 12 hours with no rest. His manager said he worked like a machine. I carry the same genes and can work tirelessly around the clock since I enjoy what I do.

My father was a workaholic. To him, his work was a drug. He used to say that the roaring sound of the rig was like Beethoven's symphony to his ears. When the rod struck water and water came bursting out with great force, his face immediately lit up with pure joy. It was an indescribable feeling to see my dad so thrilled.

My daughter and I stayed with Dad and my brother. Our digs were inconvenient; we had to share a single room. It was by no means a place for a woman with a baby. My dad's colleagues, who were sharing the room with him and my brother, were kind enough to vacate this room so he, my brother, my daughter, and I could stay there. We slept on the floor. I recall that the ceiling fan wobbled dangerously. I made a canopy for my daughter with cushions and clothes lest the ceiling fan should fall on her. Scary times!

The bathroom outside was in a pathetic state, as all the other workers used it too. I was the only woman in the group. But then, I did not care. I was with my dad and my brother, and that was all that mattered. My daughter and I were safe. I thought of the fun times when my brother and I had ridden the rig as children and stayed outdoors, the sun kissing our faces.

A month passed by. It was now time to go back home. It had been fun to reconnect with my brother; we had grown apart since our teens. Like an old habit that does not die easily, I had begun missing Andy. I was aching for him, the ache gnawing at my heart. We took the train to Hyderabad. I felt myself being drawn to Andy inexorably as the train neared Hyderabad.

We came back to live in a joint family with my mother's brothers, sisters, and mother. I didn't like it, but I had no choice. I had missed a month of college and did not know how I'd make up for that. I asked my mother if she could accompany me to the university, speak to the principal, and explain to her that I was having domestic troubles. I had to get back to reality and stop leading this nomadic life. Had I been single and independent, such a hippie life would have been quite normal. But I was married and had a daughter. I had a family to look after and had to prepare for a good future. My future and that of my daughter depended upon *me*. I couldn't afford to be reckless. I needed to straighten my act, study hard, and, most importantly, be financially independent.

My mother was tense. Of course, she was happy. But at the same time, she was afraid of Andy's reaction. She said he and his mother had come searching for me, but she had told them she did not know where I had gone. Andy and his mother said they would lodge a police complaint stating that I had kidnapped my daughter.

Utterly ridiculous, I thought. My daughter was mine and only mine. I would definitely hurt anyone who tried to take her away from me. There was no law that could punish me for going away with my daughter. I tried to console Mom. 'How can you believe such things, mummy? Do you really think they can do this?'

My mom was displeased. She was a meek, dainty lady. I had never heard her shout or get into an argument. Her reply was, 'Yes, baby. Your husband is a street fighter. He is capable of stooping to any level. We are not used to this type of behavior.'

"Yes, Mom, I know, but I can become a street fighter too! I, too, can go to any extent.'

My mom was tired of this. She thought we were creating a nuisance. She said, 'Andy came almost every other day to ask about you, and it is a matter of time before he comes again.'

Thankfully, Andy respected Mom and did not fight with her. It was only with my dad that he fought. Both were like oil and water; they could never see eye to eye. And this continued for years. They barely tolerated each other.

I thought maybe Andy was missing me and would stop his philandering. I missed him too but did not tell my parents this. I started building castles in the air again. Andy would stop drinking, he would be a changed man, he wouldn't cheat, and we would live happily ever after.

On the other hand, my parents thought that I had come back to their house for good. Little did they know that I hadn't given up on my marriage; I would still fight for Andy and I to be together. I still believe in the power of love, marriage, and family. But Andy had to be taught a lesson, I told myself. He was a spoilt brat, always drinking and whiling away his time without any sense of responsibility. *Let him come and apologize*, I thought. I would then go back to him. I did not know that, when it came to marriage, there would never be a 'happily ever after' in my life.

My dad encouraged my dream to immigrate to the USA. I was at home for almost a week, expecting Andy to show up anytime. But he did not. Another week passed. I started thinking that perhaps he did not want me or my daughter anymore. A sense of despondency took over.

The third week after we were back from Indore, we went to the university. The angry principal berated my mother and refused to give us the original certificates I had submitted to the university at the time of joining the B.Ed. Program. She chastised me. 'Domestic violence is not a situation to be treated lightly, and this is no way for both of you to behave! With a merit scholarship, you should be ashamed of yourself. You've got a free ride to college, but you are wasting it, not thinking of your future or that of your daughter, seriously.' The humiliation made me want to sink into the earth. I knew it was a wake-up call. I had been on the verge of giving up. I wasn't thinking straight.

The principal told me to resume college the next day. I was elated yet nervous. I had already missed a chunk of the course. In a few more months, the course would be over. Would I be able to make up for lost time? The principal boosted my morale. 'I know you will do it. In the short time you've been here, you have made a mark with many of the professors.' Greatly encouraged, I resumed attending classes the next day. It was difficult since I had lost so much time and did not have the required books. But somehow, the next week went by peacefully. I spent hours and hours at the library, which closed at 9 pm, and often came home late. The good thing was I did not need to rush back home to my daughter since my parents took care of her. My dad was waiting for the next drilling contract to begin and was home for a period of time. A few weeks passed peacefully, and I settled down again at my parents' home. But deep down, I was restless and sad and often cried at night. I missed Andy a lot.

He came by one evening. Surprisingly enough, despite the fact that it was 8 pm, he wasn't drunk. I was overjoyed to see him. And he, to see me. Of course, my dad was angry. He told me to ask Andy to get out and tell him I did not want to see him again.

Andy came in boldly and sat down, saying he had come to take his wife and child. I was pleased that he wasn't drunk. His assertive nature was as appealing to me then as it had been when I first met him. He looked a little thinner. He told me, 'Sharon, I am sure things will work out. Everything will be normal; just come home.' I instantly melted and told my parents I wanted to go back with him. My dad retorted, 'Baby, how can you go? This is not the right decision. You are in college; you want to go to America!' The argument went on for a bit. I usually never got into a screaming match with my father, but I did it that night, packed my bag, and left with Andy to go back to Tarnaka.

Andy's parents were not pleased to see me, but they were thrilled to see the baby. The runaway daughter-in-law was back. After hearing a bit of chastising, I settled down again. Andy was distraught. He thought he had lost me. He said, 'Don't do that again — disappear on me. I won't go out with other women. I will be faithful.'

Finally, we settled down into the old routine again. In the past two years, I realized that I was living out of my backpack, like a nomad, with a limited number of clothes. I had three or four sarees, but that was sufficient to look decent and presentable. My mother had bought me and my daughter some more clothes, and we were able to get by without looking like vagabonds.

Time with Andy passed reasonably happily. Though he did drink in the evenings, he did not beat me for a while. He spent more time with my daughter and me. My studies were going well, though making up for the missed classes was exhausting. They allowed me to take the tests I had missed, and I often worked into the wee hours of the morning. Sleep had no place in my life. I slept at 2 am or 3 am, woke up by 5 am to feed and bathe my daughter, finish some household chores, and fixed breakfast along with my mother-in-law for the family before I left for college.

By then, Andy slid back into his old ways of drinking and beating me. Slowly, we began to live almost separate lives. I could never have a discussion with him about my teaching or anything intellectual. If I tried to get him to read some of my books, he would say I was mad. Our arguments began again. I missed my dad, but I did not see him or even ask Andy if I could visit him. I was focused on getting my teaching degree and was impatient to find a job.

I was named among the top five students at the university for the B.Ed. Program, and held a distinction. I was thrilled beyond measure, and surprisingly, so was Andy! He nor his family members would ever know that I would not settle down as a teacher. I was now hungry to study further and take up a Master's degree.

But for that, I had to wait patiently. *No, so fast, not so fast*, I told myself. I was an eagle who wanted to spread her wings wide and soar high. The vast expanse of the huge sky beckoned to me. A bright future awaited me. I felt alive. The energy bubbling and bursting within me filled me with the utmost positivity.

I landed a job in less than two weeks at a high school in Habshiguda, a neighborhood of Hyderabad. My salary was decent. I loved teaching; my creativity was back. I was one of the best teachers in the school and set high standards, much to the consternation of my peers. My students loved me, and I loved them.

Andy continued drinking. The beatings were back. Sometimes, they were bad enough to send me to the hospital. The doctor there was fed up with my repeated appearances. Once, she asked me if I could feel the pain coursing through my bruised body. I looked at her stoically and said, 'I do, but my mind seems to be stronger, and I can trick myself into not feeling the pain at times.' Andy was careful not to hit me on my face. I think he was a master of how to beat someone. Perhaps he had picked this up from living like a wild child. He even knew how to put a person in a chokehold.

Luckily, he never did that to me. I saw him do it to three people in my lifetime. In one of our happier moments, he even explained to me that the rationale behind a chokehold was to simply strike terror in the heart of the other person. It was an art, he said, adding that one should never try it unless one knew when exactly to ease the pressure on the other person's windpipe.

Otherwise, you could end up killing them. Crazily in love or perhaps mad, instead of being scared, I was in awe of him when he said this.

Somehow, I had come to terms with my life. I knew Andy would not change; he'd continue to drink and abuse me. My job was to continue to study, find a good job, go to the USA, and bounce back stronger in life.

Visits to the police station took place every now and then when Andy fought with his family or his friends. I think this comes with the territory. Social drinking is acceptable, but excessive drinking is not. Andy was unrestrained and did what he pleased at all times. He never accepted social standards or norms. He had no trouble holding his drink; he didn't know when to stop. Yes, he was an alcoholic, and like all other alcoholics, I thought he needed care and love to bring him back on track. I gave him this love and care. Sometimes, I treated him the way a patient is to be treated. But all in vain.

Sometimes, he would casually speak about stabbing a person as if this was nothing. I remember the time he told me, 'You know, Sharon, when you plunge a knife into someone's guts, you have to twist and turn it in one stroke lest you should spill the guts out.' I wasn't sure if he was joking or not. I empathized with his behavior because I thought he was like this due to the lack of a proper upbringing and family support. When you live with rough friends and strangers from the age of fourteen into your late twenties, you are a child of your circumstances, I rationalized.

I tried to reason with myself that he wasn't a bad person, but someone lost between his family and friends, swinging between love and hate. His was a Jekyll-and-Hyde type of personality. Between his beatings and his remorse, I felt as if I had died and risen again, refreshed. Maybe I was tricking my brain into thinking this way. Maybe this was my coping and survival mechanism.

I took lots of Crocin and what I called the 'pretty pink tablets,' Brufen, to kill my pain every day. And the next day, I was back to teaching and being happy, as if nothing had happened. When my daughter became an adult, she started saying, 'Ma, you are normally abnormal.'

During the first week of the month, when we received our paycheck, Andy indulged us. He took our daughter and me out to our favorite haunt, Alpha Hotel, near Secunderabad railway station. I loved these once-a-month evenings away from his family. We had a few hours of peace and quiet when he did not drink on these outings. My favorite food at this restaurant was biryani and alpha pudding.

Andy thought he was being benevolent in taking us out like this since I complained that he never took us out as a family but spent every evening with his friends. When he drank with his friends in our home, I was treated like the house help. I had to provide them with snacks and dinner. When his friends left after midnight, I had to clean up after them. I felt like my dog Brownie; after the beatings, the shouting, and the hateful insults, I would pick myself up and shake everything away like Brownie would pick himself up from a puddle, shake the dust and dirty water, and walk away. What a thought! I thank God for giving me an amazingly resilient nature. I would have crumbled to dust during those tough times.

Brownie was a huge dog, though he was a puppy. He was a crossbreed. He shed tears when I cried and was more in tune with my emotions than any of the humans at home. In the beginning, when my daughter was born, he was jealous of her. Later on, he loved and guarded her. Although he belonged to Andy, he took to me once I entered this family and became mine. The connection was spontaneous. My daughter loved him and often made cooing noises when he entered the room. He often slept on my bed, and later, when my daughter was born, he resigned himself to sleeping on the floor but close to our bed. One day, someone poisoned him; the night he died was an agonizing one. I was sorrowful for days and days after that. Brownie's death was a big blow to me. He had been my only partner in my time of distress. His death created a void in my life.

Master of Science

I was working as a science teacher, having successfully completed a 3-year Bachelor of Science (B.Sc.) program and an intense B.Ed. Teaching program. Everyone at Andy's place thought I would be 'settled' by now. Little did they know that my secret visits to the Osmania University library over the past year and a half had strengthened my desire to pursue a master's degree. I wasn't sure if I could receive another merit scholarship. It seemed like an uphill task, with a child, a husband who drank and beat me constantly, and a house that was more a battlefield than a home. I knew I had to gird my loins and somehow do it.

Almost 75 thousand students applied for the entrance examination for the master's degree. Very few were offered a merit scholarship. 'Help me, God!' I prayed sincerely. I told myself that the worst that could happen was I wouldn't be accepted into the program. If I received a scholarship, I would have to pay almost nothing for the program —the equivalent of one or two US dollars. Pursuing the same program in a private college would cost me approximately Rs. 30,000 - the equivalent of 375 US dollars at today's exchange rate, which was beyond my reach. Let alone 30,000 rupees, I did not have 25 rupees- the equivalent of 50 cents in my pocket at most times! Even with a higher salary, I had to give Andy my entire earnings.

I was back to visiting second-hand bookstores and studying for the entrance examination. Andy and his parents were surprised that I wanted to study further; perhaps they had underestimated me. They didn't seem to care, thinking it was another foolish idea of mine to get yet another degree and make it to America. What they thought did not bother me. I continued to study past midnight, often wondering if I could ever get out of the mess I had landed in.

Most often, I did not eat my meals simply because I was sad and longed for Andy to focus on me and our daughter.

I took the entrance exam and went to check the results on the appointed day. The previous day, I had taken an extra-hard dose of beating from Andy. I somehow dragged myself wearily out of bed and went to work. From there, I went to the university campus at about 3 pm. I was tense and anxious. When I reached the campus, there were hundreds of people waiting to check the results of the entrance exam. Thankfully, the scorching heat had let up a bit. I had to wait in line patiently for my hall ticket. I had not eaten the entire day, and the world seemed to be spinning around me. Aggravated by the anxiety of what could be or what could not be, I began to feel faint and dizzy. The next minute, without any warning, I collapsed onto the floor.

I recall my head hitting the floor hard. I seemed to hear several voices around me. A commotion ensued, and a number of people surrounded me. A few of them gently made me sit up. Someone gave me some water and asked me if I was okay. I replied in a shaky voice, 'Yes, yes. I am fine. I did not eat.' Someone rushed and bought me a glass of sugarcane juice, which was quite popular at the university. Still dizzy, I requested someone to check on the results and let me know if I had been accepted into the master's program.

He came back after ten minutes and told me that I had been accepted and had received a merit scholarship! Unbelievable! The thrill that coursed through my veins was uplifting; my weariness left me instantly. Renewed and restored, I rushed to see the result for myself. People allowed me to pass the line and were courteous. And yes, indeed, my name was on the list of students who were selected for a merit-based scholarship.

I could not believe my eyes. I took the bus back to Tarnaka and informed Andy's parents. They did not seem to be too pleased with the result. Instead, the first thing they asked me was, 'Why are you so late?' When I explained, they said, 'Does this mean you will have to stop working for the next two years or so?' They did not see the point in studying further since I already had a job. Andy's parents admonished me that I had to stop acting like I wanted a carefree college life. I had to start being responsible, they said.

Andy wasn't too pleased either, but I guess he let it be. I told him the two years would fly by. Perhaps I could take tuition or work somewhere in the evenings and earn something. The master's program would begin in a month. By that time, I would have a plan, I told him. I was thrilled, and my heart was singing. At that time, I did not realize that I would not stop with the master's degree or that the next two years would be tumultuous, with strange experiences. My only thought was that a master's degree could be my ticket out of Hyderabad.

Andy and I continued to drift apart slowly. My master's program began at Nizam College, Osmania University. It was another intense program. I left home early and came back in the evening. During the day, Andy's parents took care of my daughter, and they were not happy about it. Andy began seeing other women and came back late in the night, drunk. The fistfights in his family and his beatings continued. I stuck to my course unfailingly; I was seeking my true North. This was the most exciting part of my life —

a ticket for my family to go abroad. I told myself this again and again.

A few months into my master's program, one night, I was exhausted but could not sleep. I was sitting in the living room and studying. My daughter was fast asleep. One of my brothers-in-law came into the living room, drunk, and began to speak to me about how Andy was ill-treating me. Uncomfortable with his presence in this state, I tried to go back to our bedroom. He accosted me. The unthinkable was happening! I was completely taken by surprise. How dare he? I thought this little man was much smaller than me in stature.

I slapped him and took him down, pinning him to the ground. *You little worm*! I thought. I was enraged, and this thought made me stronger. The adrenalin pumped into me as I pummeled him. He was much weaker than Andy and seemed very surprised by my instant retaliation. He immediately began screaming for his mother in Telugu. 'Amma, amma! Come and help me!' Andy's mom came flying down the hallway and looked at us in utter disbelief. A grown man was being beaten up by a woman inside the house! Her reaction was shock and anger. She started screaming, 'Stop! Stop! Have you gone mad? Has a demon possessed you? You witch, leave my son alone!' She began to rain blows on me. I created a terrible commotion and began screaming, too. By then, Andy's father joined the fight. He beat me with his walking stick, not knowing the cause of the fight. I ran out of the house into the open, thinking that these three could do nothing if I was outside. I was faster than them and much more agile.

Once I went out, they shut the door on me. My daughter woke up and began wailing. It was terrible. Her cries spurred me on. I tried to get back into the home, crying, 'My Christina, my Christina!' The three of them said I had been taken over by an evil spirit and had to be thrown out of the house. Disheveled and distraught, I went berserk. I began to kick the door like a mad woman. I was consumed by anger, grief, and pain. Mr. Nanda Kumar, our good neighbor, as usual, came to the rescue.

I calmed down a bit after a while and continued to sit at the gate. Andy arrived after a few hours. Seeing him, I began to weep uncontrollably. Of course, he was drunk. When he heard my tale, he could not take the atrocity. Immediately, he charged into the house. It was a fistfight again. I told Andy, 'I cannot stay here. This is unsafe for Christina and me. Take me to a separate home immediately, or I will go back to my parents.' Andy told me to pack my bags. He said he would drop me at my parents' home and resolve the situation the next day. I felt extremely relieved; this was the first time he supported me.

It was 3 in the morning. I took a small suitcase with my daughters' clothes, my clothes, my books and we left on the motorbike. In spite of the unearthly hour, my dad was overjoyed to see me. Of course, he wasn't happy to see Andy. I said tersely, 'Dad, there was a big altercation. Can I stay here until Andy sorts things out at his home?' My dad and mom asked no questions. We went inside, and Andy left for the night. Before he left, he said, 'I will come tomorrow, and we will decide what to do.'

I told my parents about the events that had taken place. They were livid with Andy's brother. My dad said, 'Baby, go to sleep. Nothing to worry at all. You have come back, and I am happy.'

Two days passed by, but Andy did not come. I was anxious by now. I did not have the courage to go back to his house after that awful fight. My dad started admonishing and counseling me again. 'Baby, you should leave him. He will never take care of you or your daughter. Focus on going to America, focus on your studies.'

'Yes,' I said, 'I am doing that, but I don't want to leave Andy.' It was not long before the irritations of staying with Mom's side of the family started to get to me: the old complaints that I was using too much water, too much gas, etc. At times like that, I wished that my parents gave their children first priority, as most other parents do. Perhaps my life would have been quite different in that case. By the way, though the person who violated me still lived in that house, he never approached me, probably out of fear of Andy. I did not feel unsafe. Moreover, by now, I was more than a handful and was full of fight. I had learned the ways of the world and knew that to survive, I had to protect myself.

Andy came after a few days. I was upset with him. He urged me to go back with him to the Tarnaka house. He said his brother was sorry and that this would not happen again. But I was done with his family; I refused to go back there and said, 'Andy, you promised me that we would live in a separate house.' He remained adamant. I could not believe this was happening to me! Not used to seeing us fight, my parents seemed to be quite shocked as well. Dad supported me and said, 'Andy, you'd better leave. She does not want to come to your home; it is not safe.'

Andy attacked my dad, and a fistfight began on the street in front of the house. My dad and Andy were both very strong. My dad was an able-bodied driller who could take on people half his age. Andy never thought my father would be a match for him. I had never seen my dad fight like this. The cops came again, and so began another spectacle. My relatives were angry since it was a street fight; they felt embarrassed. I told the cops I did not want to go with my husband since he drank, cheated on me, and beat me. In India in those days, there was no law against beating your wife.

And so, Andy left.

I continued my master's program, somehow juggling my duties as a parent and a student. My parents helped take care of my baby. Thankfully, since I had a merit scholarship, I had to spend money on buying a few books. The rest I could borrow from the British Library in Hyderabad. After college, I went there every other day to study. I would often get late while coming back home. Another few months went by this way.

One day, Andy came to meet me at Nizam College and asked me to go back home with him. I was weary of his nonsense by then and asked him if he would at least stop seeing other women, even if he would not stop drinking. He promised me that he would only if I went with him. I, too, missed him and decided to go back. Of course, my parents were angry with me: this wild swinging between the two houses was no way to lead life, they said.

I knew that. I was living like a nomad, drifting; the only stable things in my life were my child and my unwavering ambition of studying and going to the USA.

I went back to Andy's home. I was naïve to have thought that things would be better. They remained the same. I felt helpless since I had no peace at either my parents' home or my husband's home. I thought America was the place to be, and my ticket there would be my education.

Andy started seeing one woman in particular during that time and often did not come home during the night. I felt I could not go back to my parents and somehow tried to adjust to this new distressing reality. At times, I fought with him; at other times, I held my peace.

Feeling dizzy a lot, I went to see a doctor one day. Fantastic news! I was pregnant again! Andy thought I should stop going to college.

'Why?' I demanded and said, 'My pregnancy is not a disease. I can study and still be pregnant.' By now, he was drifting away from me more than ever and was seen with the other woman often. One night, we got into a fight again. He slapped me, and I fell on the edge of the wooden cot and hit my stomach. It was awful! There was blood everywhere. I was rushed to the nursing home at Sitaphal Mandi. I had a miscarriage.

I was sick for three days, shivering with fever, anger, and pain. On the fourth day, the fever broke. Andy berated me, saying it was all my fault. I wept inconsolably. The next day, I wiped away my tears and began to attend college again.

The death of my unborn child made me stronger. I had lost so much in life that I was not afraid of anything anymore. Immune to any kind of pain, I decided to get back to my routine. Though everything was chaotic at home, I was grateful that Andy's parents at least took care of my daughter when I attended college. My little one had somehow captured their hearts. I was worried that all this turmoil would affect her.

In the middle of one night the following week, Andy asked me to leave with my daughter during one of his drinking episodes. It was 2 am! I always wondered why bad things happen more during the night. Darkness always seemed to bring bad moments.

I picked up my daughter and left for my parents' home again. Since I did not have any money, I had to walk. I was numb to whatever was going on. I came to my parent's house again. *This year has been extra turbulent*, I thought. Everyone in my mom's joint family was tired of my episodes of coming and going. Some of the neighbors viewed me with disdain and would not speak to me. I was never invited to any wedding or birthday parties in my mom's or my dad's family. Not that I wanted to attend any. In general, no one in the family wanted to befriend me. Several of my extended family members ignored me and spread rumors about me as if they knew the truth. But I did not care about all this; my life was now on a different path. They continue to perpetuate these rumors even to this day.

I continued my master's program. Sometimes, I had to skip college due to the upheavals in my life. Whenever my daughter was sick, I had to stay at home and tend to her. I made up for lost time by working extra hard, often staying up late to review all the missed work of the day.

On a positive note, staying with my parents meant that I didn't need to rush back home from university. I was able to study in the university library. On certain days, my daughter would tag along with me to the laboratory and library. She had fun and my classmates liked her very much.

To the Brink and Back

A few months passed uneventfully. I was depressed. Amazingly, in spite of everything going against me, I was able to focus on my studies. I buried myself in the master's program. I loved the atmosphere at the university. It was here that I found some peace. I was oblivious to the pain caused by a husband who did not care for his wife or child. Andy came to the university several times and made it a point to whiz past the bus stop at specific times he knew I'd be there. He kept tabs on my whereabouts.

Somehow, he always knew about my arrival and departure at the university but never approached me. Sometimes, there would be a woman riding pillion with him; those were the extra-difficult days for me. Seeing my husband in the arms of another woman was too much to handle. In those days, sleeplessness was my only ally. I spent sleepless nights, but for a different reason- I channeled my rage into my work and studied throughout the night. It was only at dawn that I would catch a few hours of sleep before leaving for college again. Strangely, I never felt exhausted. On the contrary, I felt energized and continued chugging along.

A few more months went by. Andy stopped passing by the university bus stop. At home, I felt lonely, though my daughter kept me happy and comforted me. She was my solace. She was almost three years old now. Much like me, she too was a fast learner, brimming with curiosity. Scientific research confirms that, on average, a small child asks 300 questions a day. My daughter was most inquisitive. I enjoyed answering her questions, and her inquisitiveness sharpened my grey cells.

The week before Christmas, Andy came to the university with this other woman I had often seen riding with him. Both of them accosted me while I was walking to my class. The woman demanded that I sign an agreement for mutual divorce since I was no longer interested in continuing to live with Andy. They handed me the court documents. I was completely flummoxed but somehow maintained a cool expression. Keeping my nerve, I took the documents and tore them up.

Giving the two of them a stony gaze, I spat out, 'Andy, here, take the documents,' and threw the little bits of paper up into the air with utter disdain.

Obviously, they did not take this audacity well. I said to Andy, 'This is between you and me. Who is the third person to talk to me? I have nothing to say to her.'

Jumping to her defense, Andy shot back, 'She's not a third person. You are refusing to come back home with me. Will you come back and be a good wife? No, you won't. I have given you several chances to come back, but you are adamant. I have decided to move on with my life!'

His heartless words shattered me, but I continued to maintain a cool demeanor. 'OK, then. Send the divorce papers to my home. Let's fight this out in court. I am signing nothing now. And you won't get the child either since *you* are the one wanting a divorce, not me.'

The woman kept interfering in our conversation, although I refused to acknowledge her presence. I ignored her like she was a fly on the wall. I wanted to lash out at Andy, but I valued my reputation at the university and wore a calm demeanor. I started walking rapidly away from the university building. Both of them followed me, and suddenly, this woman started beating me with her purse and demanding, 'Sign the papers, sign the divorce papers! How dare you tear them up? We want to live our life.' That drove me crazy. Immediately, I began beating her. She was like putty in my hands. *Another small creature*, I thought.

I did not expect that Andy would come to her rescue. The blows began to rain on me. I hit the ground instantly; he was way too strong for me. Arms flailing around, hair disheveled, I felt the dust in my mouth. I tried to leave the university campus. My only thought was that I would be kicked out of the program. Several students gathered around, watching us. I wanted to disappear out of shame.

The watchman came running to break up the fight and threw us out of the campus. Shaking with anger and shame, I boarded a bus home. Andy and the woman left on his motorbike. I cried throughout the 45-minute bus journey. Everyone on the bus was staring at me, but I couldn't care less. No one asked me what was wrong or what had happened. I felt I should end my life, that there was no peace at all. I felt helpless and thought my daughter would be better off without me.

Everything was hazy and dark. My head was throbbing with pain. I don't remember how I visited three medical pharmacies and bought sleeping tablets. I went to three different pharmacies so I would not arouse any suspicion. The excruciating physical pain and intense emotional trauma had benumbed me. There was no way I could continue living like this. I decided that this shame must end.

I sat down for a while at the bus stop near my parents' home. Mad with anger, grief, and pain, my mind knew no rational thought. I had thought people who took their own lives were spineless, but now I was about to go their way. Truly, I had lost my mind in anger and frustration. Even today, I shudder to think of those moments.

I bought some water, gulped down the tablets, and took enough to be considered a massive dose. My system was filled with poison, and my brain was devoid of all rationality; I walked home quickly. It was a ten-minute walk home from the bus stop. My maternal grandmother was at home. My daughter and my dad had gone outside. My mom was at work. I collapsed on the bed, thinking this was the end of my life.

When I opened my eyes, I was in the ICU of Gandhi Hospital in Secunderabad. Three days had passed. I was confused, weak, and dizzy. I did not understand anything. The last I remembered was that I was going to die. Later on, I came to know that I had begun frothing and vomiting in the unconscious stupor that I had slipped into. My dad had come back home at the right time. He immediately rushed me to the emergency ward of the hospital, where I remained for several days. My dad did not leave my side even for a minute. What a terrible thing I had done to myself while putting my parents and my daughter at a huge risk! I felt disgusted at my behavior and agonized over this for the next few days.

My parents were overjoyed to see me recover. My dad never asked me a thing, but I told him what had happened. He consoled me in the most soothing manner, patting my head gently. He said, 'Don't worry, baby, everything will be fine. You should not give up. You're a big, strong girl now.' I asked for my daughter, but they could not bring her since I hung between life and death in the intensive care unit. No one at home was given the exact details about what had happened. The rumor mills started churning again.

Five days later, my daughter visited me. She came to see me after I was moved to the general ward of the hospital. She came running to me with her large eyes and cried, 'Mommy!' and hugged me with all her might. I felt her warm little hands around me, and my world lifted again. I cursed myself for doing such a disgusting thing and leaving this child to the world. I had to live for her, I thought, as I spent a fortnight in the hospital.

I returned home a mellow person. I had had much to think about during those days in the hospital. No one in the family made a mention of what had befallen me. They snickered behind my back. During that time, my dad was my greatest strength and biggest source of encouragement. I stayed home for another three weeks. I was anxious that I would perhaps lose my seat at the university- I did not have the courage to go back. After all, hundreds of students had witnessed the unusual fight, almost like in the movies. I felt ashamed.

I told my dad I wasn't sure what to do. He said he would speak to the Head of my department and assured me that no one would make fun of me. He said he would accompany me to the university for a few days. 'Give it a try, baby. It's a matter of your life and future. Very few get an opportunity like this, with a merit scholarship and all. It's a once-in-a-lifetime chance! God has been merciful to you and has given you the talent and the brains. Not many have the intelligence you are bestowed with.' His words boosted my morale and renewed my confidence.

I went back to continue my master's program. My dad came with me to the university every day with my daughter, and they spent some time with me during the lunch break. Everyone eyed me curiously, but no one said anything. I tried to forget the dreadful episode and was able to move past the embarrassment. The only reminder of the whole sordid affair was the physical trauma, which lasted almost two months. During that time, I felt weak and sometimes dizzy, especially when I stood for a long time at the bus stop. My dad kept encouraging me, and by the time I entered the third month after my hospitalization, I was bouncing back with renewed enthusiasm, intensely focused on my studies.

Sadly, Andy never came to see me, even when I was admitted to the hospital and fighting for my life. I thought that was the end of everything. I would have to spend my entire life with my daughter for company.

Despite all the trauma, I passed the first year of the master's program with flying colors. I was now well into my second and final year. Life continued as usual. By now, my sights were set on the PhD program. I found that I was fiercely ambitious. Nainamma's words, 'Education is the wealth that no one can take away from you,' echoed in my head. I have passed on her wisdom to my children and trust that they will pass it on to *their* children.

Another year passed. I saw Andy once in a while, but he never approached me. Neither did I venture to speak to him. I never saw him again with that woman and had no way of knowing what had happened. That fortnight in the hospital had changed a lot for me and in me. The young mother, who was rushed to the hospital after an overdose of sleeping pills, had come out a transformed person. As the poison of the sleeping pills was drained from my body, I felt like it cleansed me of all the demons from my past. No more was I the romantic fool who would stoop so low as to attempt suicide for a man. I refused to degrade myself in the name of love. My life was mine. I would write my own story and not allow another person to hold the strings of my life. The girl who went into the ICU and the one who came out of it were two very different people.

I was determined to become successful. The pain numbed my heart, but I got used to feeling this way; it was now a way of life, and I learned to embrace it. The pain had made me and my heart go stone cold. It was now a vital part of me. We had become one. It was my best friend; it strengthened me and gave me courage.

In time, I felt that my heart was intact again, and I started healing. Sometimes, though, I went to Andy's workplace with my daughter. When I was extremely troubled, my daughter and I sat at the bus stop and waited for Andy to whizz by. Just seeing him somehow calmed my troubled spirit. Strange, very strange, indeed.

The man who was the cause of all the pain and trauma in my life could also ease me of the same pain. I did not understand myself.

At times, I'd sit at the bus stop, waiting for the merest glimpse of Andy. Maybe I saw this as a reminder of the hurt and pain he had caused me and, at the same time, of how he had loved me. Sometimes, he would see us, rev up his motorbike engine, and zip away. My daughter and I would get up and leave, too. My daughter was too young to understand what was happening.

My parents' support during that period was immense. I felt strengthened by their love at that crucial point in my life. I'm grateful to them for that.

The fact that I was in my final year of the master's degree was exciting. I felt quite accomplished. I had a double Bachelor's and was soon getting a Master's degree. Life was looking rosy in spite of my troubles. To support my daughter and myself financially, I began teaching at a high school tutorial in the evenings on alternate days. My salary was low. Still, it was better than nothing. Thankfully, all the books were borrowed from the university library, and I did not need to pay any tuition fees as I was a merit scholar. My parents took care of our food, rent, and clothes during this time.

I completed final examinations for my Master's program and waited for the results. I was excited to know that I had a chance to apply for the PhD program. I started visiting the main university campus again, which was different from the one where I had studied for my Master's. This campus was close to Andy's home. In preparation for my PhD entrance exam, I would have to select a topic of interest and read up on it before I joined the program. I often haunted the campus, visited the library, and drank sugarcane juice, my favorite summer drink. One beautiful summer afternoon, I was in the campus library when Andy showed up with his disarming charm. Almost a year had gone by since we had last spoken, though we saw each other when he whizzed past on his motorbike.

We talked and talked like nothing had happened. Once again, we began to meet each other rather stealthily on weekdays. I was especially careful not to take my daughter out with me on those days. It was strange. We were still husband and wife, and yet, it felt like we were unmarried and dating. He said he was sorry about what had happened and that it had been a ploy to get me back. That is why he came to the University with the other woman. Andy said, 'Why do you think you never saw me with her after that day? I wanted you back, and I wanted you at any cost, even if it meant hurting you.'

Really? So, you beat me for that? Bizarre logic, I thought. I don't know whether I believed him or not. I might have been suspicious, but I let the disturbing thought pass. We met for coffee or snacks and often sat together at lunch in the university gardens. It was indeed fun. I could not imagine telling my dad about the latest developments in my love life, and neither could Andy imagine taking me back to his home. Two months passed this way.

The final results of the Master's program were released. I had topped the university again and earned a 'Distinction' grade. I was ready for the next step of working towards my doctorate degree.

Oh, the excitement was heady! I told Andy we must go to America and start a new life there with our daughter. He seemed to be pleased about this, and our little dates continued. I think I was actually happy during that time because I had the best of both worlds. I could meet Andy often but did not have to suffer his beatings, witness his drinking, or live with my in-laws. At the same time, I could live with my parents, who cared for me and my daughter. I was a free spirit, ready to take wing and bask in the glow of what I thought was love. I guess I was being a bit selfish, too, enjoying being carefree with my parents and spending time with my husband at the same time. Was I indeed the love fool who thought life was a happy romance? Such dreams do not behoove an intelligent person. But my heart and the mind were in two different stratospheres, each one having nothing to do with the other.

Now, it was time to find a job. With a Master's degree, I could easily find a job in a college as a lecturer. The thought was exciting since I loved teaching. I began applying to colleges for the position of lecturer, one of them being Wesley Junior College. The selection process and the competition were intense. The applicants had to take an examination and hold a demonstration lecture for the selection committee members. I hoped I would get a job there!

Going Back

Tired of meeting me on the sly, Andy asked me to go back home with him. I was tense about living with him and his family and afraid to inform my parents. This dilemma continued for a month. After that, I mustered up the courage to inform my parents that I had been meeting Andy, and both of us wanted to reunite. I told them we were hopeful that this time, our marriage would be successful. All hell broke loose again.

My parents were opposed to this move and reminded me of all the incidents that had happened in the past. They admonished me and reminded me that I was now fully qualified to be a lecturer and that Andy wanted me back because he wanted a wife with a handsome salary. I didn't think that was true, but who knows? They may well have been right. It was true that Andy never cared about education. In fact, he thought it was a waste of time. There had been several times when I was studying when he switched off the light, saying the electric bill was too high and that there was no need for me to study. Furious, I had studied by torchlight just to spite him. Sometimes, he grabbed the torchlight from me! And we engaged in another fight.

My memory, as usual, was short-lived when it came to Andy. Eventually, with much grief, I bid my parents goodbye and said I would come to visit soon. We went back to Andy's home. I was tense and nervous, but surprisingly, Andy's parents were receptive to my return. I did stay clear of my brother-in-law, though, and I never really spoke to him for several years. He still drank as usual, and the brothers still continued to fight. Sometimes, Andy's dad would also be dragged into their brawls in an effort to bring them under control. It was amazing to see how this family lived, but anyway, I wasn't bothered about it. I was focused on keeping my job and preparing for the PhD entrance exam. It takes nearly a year of preparation, given how tough the exam is.

Within two weeks of my return to Andy's home, there was fantastic news. I received a job offer to work as a lecturer in Zoology at Wesley Junior College. The timings were perfect: classes began at 7.45 am and ended at noon. That would give me ample time to prepare for the PhD entrance exam in the afternoon. Of course, it would be tight since I would have to travel by bus from home to Wesley, then rush to take another bus to the university library to study in the afternoon and take another bus in the evening to come home. I was ready to do this. This was the hand of the Almighty upon me again.

My routine was simple, though tough. Rising early in the morning, I would prepare breakfast with my mother-in-law and tend to my daughter before leaving for work. My daughter was now in kindergarten, so it was easier than when she had been an infant.

Whenever I saw Andy drinking, I told myself it would be temporary; we would soon be in the States, and he would change. I wasn't clear what kind of a future we had, but whatever it was, I was sure it would be wonderful. Andy often beat me, but I was too ashamed to go back to my parents.

Sometimes, Andy threw my daughter and me out of the house, and we slept on the cold stone verandah. In the wee hours of the morning, he would call us back inside, saying, "Don't fight with me when I am drinking. I cannot control myself." The day after a beating, he was extra nice to me and would say 'I love you' several times. I learned to be stoic about all this and trained myself to tune this out of my mind. I think perhaps, during that time, I was thriving on misery. Perhaps that is why I kept returning to the same hideous life again and again. No sane person would have chosen to stay with Andy and take his shameful treatment. But I did. Was I insane? I don't know. I took to wearing a saree even at night and never a nightdress because who knew when I would be thrown out and would have to sleep outside?

I was thrilled to be teaching in a college. My students loved me, and this meant the world to me.

As always, I was giving my entire salary to Andy, who in turn paid some of this to his father as our share of the household expenses. He then rationed out a little money to me for the bus fare. Even a cup of tea or a snack outside was off-limits. "Isn't there food at home?" Andy would ask me whenever I asked for some pocket money.

In a few months, I was pregnant again. At the same time, I was diagnosed with tuberculosis and had to turn to my father for help. He took me to the government hospital. Treatment was free there. We couldn't afford to go to a private hospital. Tuberculosis was looked down upon by society, so people who had it kept it hush-hush. Luckily for me, the doctors caught it on time; I didn't have to be quarantined. The doctors said I had to take medicines for two years. That was mainly because I did not eat properly every day and was pregnant.

I miscarried for the third time. But this third experience was not as traumatic physically as the second one. I seemed to recover within a few days and was able to work and study.

Even miscarriages, it seemed, had become business as usual in my life. The second miscarriage had taken place a year earlier, though, during that time, Andy didn't beat me. The miscarriages scarred me deeply. Andy kept drifting away from me; his attitude, behavior, and lifestyle remained unchanged. The two things that make a woman die from within are sexual abuse and the loss of a child. I had encountered both several times. I was alive on the outside but dead inside. There was a void in me. Prayer filled that void and made me hold on to the thread of hope and, therefore, life.

Andy didn't allow me to meet my dad, but I did meet him on the sly at the university. He brought me snacks and food. I would eat them and sneak some back home to my daughter as little treats. On the days when Andy came to know that I had met my dad, I would get an extra dose of beating. My dad still wanted me to leave Andy, but at times, he let it be. I think he knew I was now beyond the point of turning back and would stay to fight it out. He didn't understand my attitude. For that matter, nor did I.

Another Day at Wesley College

My daily routine was wearing me down. Sometimes, due to the nocturnal beating, I could not wake up and reach college on time the next morning. If you reported late for work thrice a month, you were marked 'tardy,' and a day's pay was deducted. This happened to me as well. When I came back home with a day's salary deducted from my paycheck, Andy was furious. He thought I had kept the money to myself and beat me. My explanation of what had happened fell on deaf ears. I was in physical and emotional agony.

I could not go to work the next day and had to take a sick day. I nursed my bruised body from the night's beating and felt quite weak. I was able to rest a little and spend time with my daughter that day. Andy came back home late that night; he did not say much. The next day, I felt better, and I went to work. As always, I went into the principal's room, wished her, 'Good morning, Ma'am,' signed the register, and went to the staff room. Everyone was staring at me incredulously and refused to speak with me. I wondered if I had something on my saree. Was something wrong with my face? Or had I *done* something wrong? *What now*, I thought.

I asked one of my colleagues, "What happened? I took a sick day! Is that a problem? Did the principal say something?" She replied, "Your husband came yesterday, fully drunk, and yelled at the principal for deducting your salary. He came with a few friends who looked like thugs; they made a commotion. The timing was bad; all the students were leaving since classes were over for the day. The lone security guard could not contain the commotion. After threatening the principal, your husband left."

My blood froze. My heart was pounding. I must have looked pale as a ghost. Choking on my own words, I stammered, "I…I wasn't here…he…he never said anything to me about this!"

She shrugged.

I ran out of the staff room and went to the principal's office to apologize. I thought I would be fired. I pleaded with her, "Ma'am, I did not know anything about this. I am so sorry about the debacle."

The principal was petrified. She immediately said, "Sharon, your husband came and created a commotion. All the students saw what happened. He was yelling outside my office. I was following the rule of the college where I had to deduct a day's salary last month. But your husband…" she ran out of words.

She then continued, "I never knew he was such a raucous, uncouth fellow! I am shocked that you even live with him. I will not deduct your salary henceforth. Go back to your class." I rushed back to the staff room, terribly embarrassed and shaken but happy that I did not lose my job. I went back to class and began teaching as usual.

After that day, the principal never said a word to me whenever I was tardy. *Funny, Andy's behavior has come in handy for once*, I thought, and how violence can sometimes protect you. Of course, I did not abuse this new-found power and protection. I wanted to do my best at work, as before, and be a lecturer who loved her students and whose students loved her.

Our monetary situation continued to be tight. In the evenings, I began to teach at a coaching center for students who were preparing for the medical entrance exam. The job at Wesley did not pay much, and the money I earned from teaching at this coaching center was extra valuable. Every minute of every day of mine was accounted for; I hardly had a minute to sit at leisure or think about my life.

I always wondered why Andy was so unhappy with me. But then, right and wrong held no meaning for him. According to him, everything he said or did to me was because I never understood him or his needs, and everything was done out of love. I sometimes wondered if it was my fault that he was this way. We never had much to discuss or speak about — nothing in common. When we were not fighting, we mostly talked about money and other mundane daily matters. I was lonely in this marriage, but I held on to the hope that one day things would improve. I reminded myself of the vows I had taken to stay with him in sickness and in health. I told myself that he was sick in a sense and that he would get better. We would prevail, we would rise, we would raise our kids to be better people.

Heartbreak

December 5th was a cool morning. I clearly remember the pale pink saree I wore that day. Upon reaching college that morning, I realized that I had forgotten the lesson plan for my classes at home.

Reluctantly, since I had very little money, I took a quick autorickshaw ride back home. I was cringing at the thought of spending the extra money. When I reached home, I was surprised to see Andy's motorbike parked there.

Strange, I thought, since he had gone to work early in the morning. I did not knock on the door; we usually left the backdoor open, so I entered the house through it. Andy's parents were not at home; there was an unreal silence. Confused, I went to our room. The door was closed but not bolted. The thought that Andy could be fully drunk and sleeping inside sent me into an orbit of panic. I pushed open the door.

What I saw made me turn to stone. That memory is etched in my heart even to this day, though the hurt and pain have dulled. Don't they say that wounds heal, but the scars remain? I don't think I'll ever be able to erase that image from my mind.

Andy was with another woman. In *our* bedroom! Both were in an extremely compromising position. That sight seared my spirit and cut me to the bone. I could not react immediately. Everything moved in slow motion. Strangely, I wasn't angry. I felt my heart crush into a thousand pieces, and an ocean of sadness swept over me. A darkness that I could not comprehend entered and engulfed me completely.

I closed the door carefully, gently grabbed my lesson plan, and left the house. The two of them had heard and seen me. I walked away rapidly, almost running blindly. No tears! I could feel my shallow breaths and the pounding of my heart.

By the time I reached the bus stop, Andy overtook me since he was on his motorbike. He was angry and began to hurl abuses at me, demanding to know why I came back home.

I was too shocked to retaliate. I didn't have the usual stamina to fight. I seemed to have lost my spirit and was in despair. All I could say was, "Andy, go home. I have to go to college. I will come back in the evening, and we can talk then."

My apparent calmness startled him, and he left.

I felt dead that day. The so-called fiery passion of love that I had felt for him vanished. I experienced the feeling of 'falling out of love' that people talk about.

I was now in hell. But strangely, it did not feel as terrible as I had thought.

That evening, I came back home. There was no sign of tears, anger, or despair now that the day had passed. I was amazed at the lack of emotion. I did not want to go back to my parents. I had to stay at Andy's place, no matter what. I was, after all, my own defender, untouchable in my heart and spirit. No one could conquer me.

And then, I had *her*. My sweet little girl. The only beacon of light in the long tunnel. She lit my life up. I wondered what kind of thoughts floated in her mind. Children live without a care, don't they? When she slept, she often smiled. I marveled at her innocence. They say that little ones, when they smile in their sleep, go up to heaven and play with the angels. They wake up when they decide to come back to Earth.

I asked Andy's mother, "Aunty, how come Andy is bringing this woman to our home? Has he become so bold that he is unafraid of his own parents, too? He has no respect for elders!"

She replied, and I don't think I was shocked to hear her say this; nothing about them shocked me anymore, "Yes. You have no time for him — always working and studying. What else would a man do?" Wow! I realized that the rumors were true. People on the street gossiped that he brought this woman home when I went to college.

Fuming, I snapped, "Do you know how disgusting this is? It's one thing to know your husband is cheating on you. But seeing it from up close is something else. And to know that his parents support him. Well…in my heart, I have died. I don't think I can ever recover from this blow."

Andy came home in the evening. His mother told him that I had argued with her. It didn't take him a minute to start unleashing his blows upon me. I took all his beatings without any reaction.

The pain my body was feeling was not more than the pain he had inflicted on my heart. He beat me more than usual that day. I lay there like a dead person, allowing him to do whatever he wanted.

Finally, spent, he left me alone.

The United States of America, at that moment, had become a human being to me. A person I yearned for and wanted to elope with. I began to slowly fall in love again, not with a person but with a country. A country where I could find myself again. I thought I would elope with the United States, and that would teach these people a fine lesson. I had my little girl, my academic ambition, and my career. That was enough to take me to a far-off land of magic and peace.

The days passed. Whenever he was drunk, Andy beat me. Sometimes, he also forced himself upon me. Those nights, I simply lay there, motionless. This disgusted him; I was no longer participating in our act of being man and wife. In mind and body, I distanced myself from him.

He immediately felt this change; this infuriated him. He said, "I can have any woman I want! What is wrong with you? I don't understand you! Why have you changed?" I did not fully understand this drastic change. The man I had loved so passionately and to whom I had given my heart and soul did nothing to my heart now. My heart felt like an impenetrable fortress.

The strangest thing happened. Though he did not stop his drinking or beating, he was determined to tame me in an odd way. I am not sure if he took it as a challenge and began spending a little more time with me. At times, he was even benevolent. He took us to Alpha Hotel for dinner or to Paradise restaurant to eat my favorite biryani.

I later came to know that the other woman had demanded that he leave me. He had refused to do so, and that was the end of things between them.

I felt I had had enough pain in me to last a lifetime. "This too shall pass," I told myself, and death shall take this tired body to its final place of rest, where no pain shall capture my body or spirit.

Towards PhD

Everything seemed like a show, something that was happening to someone else. This supposition made me stronger. Some people pitied me, some hated me, and some loved me when they came to know my story. I did not complain to anyone, but somehow, people got wind of what was happening in my life.

Andy was a force to contend with, with no fear of anything or anyone. I would wistfully think that, but for his alcoholism, he'd have been an amazing person. If only he had used his drive and assertiveness in the right way.

Both of us were stubborn and poles apart. Each one of us tried to conquer the other. At times, I felt it was pointless — a battle that could never be won. But at other times, I was suffused with hope and gave the relationship my best shot.

Once in a while, when I couldn't bear to see him sinking, I renewed my strength and, like an eagle, tried to pull him out of his dark self. I made excuses for him in my mind and blamed the company he kept for his behavior. I realized later that I was wrong to think this way. A person can always, always change their bad behavior and circumstances with their desire and will power.

Andy tried hard to win his mother's affection but in vain. Curious! Both of us were pining for love from someone, but we never got it. He yearned for his mother's affection. But to her, her other children were dearer than him. Sadly and strangely, both of us found solace in our own unhappiness. Was this one reason we came together and probably understood each other on a certain level? In that strange, sad state that we shared, we felt united as husband and wife.

Like I said earlier, when my daughter stepped into her teens, she pointed out that our life was abnormally normal. This brutal truth startled me. She was absolutely right! I am able to see that my daughter's young eyes could see everything in its stark reality. Unlike me, she was not wearing any filter. She was not blinded by love.

Andy took great pride in my education. And yet, his low self-esteem made him try to tame my spirit. Sometimes, when he beat me, I cried out impulsively, 'You cannot touch me!' There were times when I intentionally goaded him on, too. This used to make him feel taunted, and he would beat me mercilessly.

My mantra was, 'This too shall pass.' Over the years, this became the leitmotif of my life, an iron rod I held on to and drew strength from. How many nights have I repeated this chant in my head, over and over again, and fallen asleep!

Andy told me he had stopped his philandering ways. That was a relief. I was still suspicious, given his track record, but I never caught him red-handed after that incident. I sincerely wanted to believe him, but my heart would not completely trust him. After all, he had wreaked havoc many a time. On the contrary, *he* was extremely suspicious of me for no reason and kept tabs on me. He would question my movements.

That year, we had to move from the huge home my father-in-law owned to a much smaller one. He was selling the big house to a builder. In the new house, everybody was in everybody else's face, and the drinking and fights only worsened. After our move, Mr. Nanda Kumar, our good and friendly neighbor in Tarnaka, wasn't there to break up the fights anymore.

Andy bought me a small moped with his own savings. This cut my commute time considerably and made it very convenient for me. It was a red Sunny. I sped away on it to college in the morning, rushed to the university in the afternoon, came back home, tended to my daughter, and then rushed to the coaching institute for two hours. I then came back to cook, clean, and get ready for the next day.

Although my daughter did not need a private tutor, I engaged one to keep her from playing on the streets all the time. She was now in school and led a busy life, too. She was back from school at 3.30 pm and would attend her tuition class in the evening.

In the midst of all this came some fantastic news. I was accepted into the PhD program. Another dream of mine was realized! I was jubilant and even more determined now.

The PhD program was a great help to fight the demons in my life. At that time, Dr. Vasantha Chary, my guide and supervisor, did me a great favor by providing me with the chemicals needed for the experiments. I had to buy the other materials for the experiments myself. Since I did not receive a stipend from the university for the PhD program, I was compelled to use a certain amount from my salary. This was not burdensome to me since it was about 5 dollars a month, in today's value. All the other materials and chemicals were covered by the University Grants Commission grant that my guide received.

Andy accused me of receiving a stipend and hiding the fact from him. He said all PhD students were given a stipend. I told him this was not true, but he didn't believe me. He went to the university and created a scene again, demanding to know if I was being paid a stipend or not! He accosted Dr.

Chary. Dr. Chary handled him rather sternly and told him off. The next day, she told me, 'Your program has nothing to do with his behavior. The next time your husband comes to the University, it will not be tolerated. I will be forced to complain to the police about him.' I respect Dr. Chary for her understanding and am grateful to her for helping me through the doctorate program.

After that episode, Andy didn't come to the university again for the entire duration of my PhD program.

I was very excited about my experiments in the lab. I did them with great enthusiasm, though it was hard since I was perpetually exhausted. Even as I was studying for my doctorate, I continued teaching at Wesley College. When Wesley had vacations, I was able to dedicate myself fully to the PhD program, working double-time on my experiments. My daughter, too, had her summer vacation at the same time, and she accompanied me to the university.

When exhaustion benumbed me, I would sit in the university gardens and look at my daughter running around the park happily. I enjoyed her company immensely and looked forward to this time with her.

A few months into my PhD program, I found out that some of my experiments and samples were being tampered with. Months of precious time and hard work had been wasted! I could not understand what was happening; it was that none of my experiments worked. Finally, one of my classmates informed me that the chemicals and reagents I prepared and stored in the refrigerator were being tampered with by some of my other classmates. I was appalled!

The treachery of these culprits made me feel abused and violated. The nightmare repeated itself a few times. I found myself being pushed to the wall. I complained to Dr. Chary. She admonished everyone and would not hear more of this. Since we had no proof, we could not identify the culprit.

I felt terrible that someone could do this to me. Perhaps one or more classmates were driven by jealousy and spite because I excelled academically and generally kept to myself. *How easy it is to judge another person*, I thought. Nobody understood that I kept to myself because I was actually sad most of the time and busy in my own world. My priorities and problems weighed me down and wore me out. I had no friends to confide my fears or dreams.

It was a relief that I managed to work, study, and take care of my daughter. I struggled from lack of sleep most of the time; my body ached from work and Andy's beatings. I had no time to think about all this and plodded on.

The more pain Andy and life inflicted upon me, the higher I soared and the freer my mind felt. I knew that, with every passing day, I was inching closer to my dream of a wonderful life in the United States.

My Son is Born

Marvelous news — I was pregnant again!

I was overjoyed! I wanted to have many children! I looked forward to the arrival of this baby. My doctor wasn't too pleased since I had been advised by doctors earlier not to get pregnant, given my frail health. I vowed to try to eat better and take my vitamins on time, even if this wasn't easy.

I credit the birth of my son to the Almighty. He and my dad were my sources of strength and support during this pregnancy. When my dad came to know that I was pregnant, he started bringing me food at the university campus every afternoon. He came on his Vespa and paid the watchman to deliver the food to me to my lab. When Andy came to know about this, he was livid but did not beat me. My dad continued to deliver food for six months. I'm grateful to him for this. I did not feel guilty when I sometimes gobbled up twice the amount of good food, more for the nourishment of the growing child. I was scared, having miscarried thrice and having had tuberculosis, although I was cured by then.

I knew that this child, too, like my daughter, would bring much joy into our lives. As the months went by and I came closer to my delivery date, I became increasingly tired. I had a minor scare one day when I could not feel the movements of the baby. I rushed to the doctor, who recommended an ultrasound scan. It was a crying shame to pay 600 rupees for the ultrasound — almost three-fourths of my salary at Wesley College! Andy paid these costs. The scan showed that the baby was fine and that it was a boy. 'It's a boy, it's a boy!' Andy exclaimed gleefully.

The doctor said I was tiring myself too much and I needed more rest. But when could I rest? I had to be on my toes from dawn to dusk and well into the night. The baby was due during the summer vacation when college would be closed. The examinations in college took a toll on me. Andy neglected me, as usual, and I was left to fend for myself. His late nights and drinking continued; however, he spared me the beatings, at least temporarily, knowing that I was carrying a son. This was so typical of the culture in India. The male child is prized and presumed to continue one's legacy, while the girl child is often neglected. Predictably, Andy's parents took better care of me this time. I informed Andy that once the baby was born, I wanted to stay with my parents for some time. That way, I would get some rest. Andy agreed. My parents lived in Golconda, which was quite a distance away from us and on the outskirts of the city of Hyderabad.

During this time, another dispute arose. Andy began to fight with his parents about the division of their property. He felt slighted; he thought his siblings were getting the lion's share in the division. I had no say in the matter, nor did I care. Andy's parents were secretive about the details of the division of the property. As usual, they treated Andy like a stepchild. They kept many other matters from us, too, leading to arguments and misunderstandings between Andy and his family members.

My mother's birthday fell on June 30. I celebrated it at my parent's place and returned to Andy's place that night. Andy's mother did not speak to me that night. I did not care; I went straight to bed, a bit relieved that Andy had gone to work and would be back home the next day after collecting his salary.

The next day, this continued, and Andy's mother and father refused to speak to me. I asked his mother, 'What has happened, Aunty? Are you angry that I came late from my mom's birthday party yesterday? Surely you can understand.' She continued to ignore me. Andy had not come back from work. I was feeling very uneasy. I asked Andy's father, 'Uncle, can you tell me what happened? Andy has not come back, and Aunty refuses to speak to me.' Peeved, his dad said, 'Ask your husband what happened. He went to his sister's house and made a commotion, kicking the door down and then verbally abusing them. He went on and on about the division of property and accused her of not giving him his share. How will we show our faces to our son-in-law now? Shocked, I said, 'I didn't know any of this'.

I marched into the kitchen and asked my mother-in-law, 'Aunty, is it my fault that Andy created a nuisance at his sister's house? If that's why you don't want to speak to me, so be it.'

At around 7 pm that evening, I began to feel physically uneasy. Andy had not returned yet. My back began to ache, and I could feel the waves of pain sweeping over my frail body. I knew this was the beginning of labor. I rushed to my mother-in-law and told her the baby was coming. She did not seem to care. She said, 'That's not possible. Isn't your due date three weeks away?' 'Yes, Aunty,' I said, 'but I can feel the pain. It's awful, and it keeps coming and going. Can you take me to the doctor now?'

The pain grew stronger; I knew I had to go to the hospital. I told my mother-in-law to accompany me since I could not drive myself on my tiny moped.

To my consternation, she refused, saying she had to visit her daughter and that it really wasn't anything I should be concerned about. She left! My daughter and my father-in-law were at home with me. My father-in-law was in a panic; we didn't have a phone at home, and there was no way to communicate with either Andy or my parents. My father-in-law was a heart patient; his eyes were failing, and he rarely went out. I told him I couldn't wait anymore, or I might have the baby right there. 'When Andy returns, ask him to come to Krishnamurthy Nursing Home,' I said. I packed a few clothes, told my father-in-law to take care of my daughter, and walked to the crossroads, which was around five minutes away. When I got into an autorickshaw, it was 9 pm.

The autorickshaw driver was a bit disturbed when he saw me fully pregnant and in pain. He drove as fast as he could. Then, an unimaginable thing happened. The railway gate at Sitaphal Mandi was closed to traffic since that was the time most of the trains were crossing. Fifteen minutes went by. My panic grew. The driver seemed to be in greater panic! He asked me to get out of his auto, saying he could not be responsible for the birth of a child or for any mishap that might occur to me. I got out of the autorickshaw weeping. A few passersby rushed up to me and asked me what happened. I told them. Immediately, a few of them lifted me and carried me across the railway tracks. I have a vague memory of reaching Krishnamurthy Nursing Home and getting myself admitted there. What an ordeal!

It was almost 10 pm. There was no doctor on duty at the hospital at that time. However, the chief nurse, Ratnamma, was on duty. She was very kind to me. Seeing my condition, she calmed me down. She said, 'Control yourself. The pains haven't peaked yet. It will be a long night. You have to conserve your energy.' She did not know that I was crying from the sheer relief of having made it to the hospital on time.

I calmed down a bit. They put me in a bed. Through the night, I was in a pain-filled haze. The pain this time seemed to be worse than that I had felt during the delivery of my daughter. I was lonely. I prayed to the Almighty for strength.

My son arrived at 3 am in the morning. When a baby arrives, the first thing any mother wants to hear is its cries. My little one did not cry. I was almost ready to leap out of the operating table in fear. Ratnamma yelled at me, 'Are you mad? Hang on, we haven't cut the umbilical cord!' I was screaming, 'Why isn't he crying? Why isn't he crying? Is he okay?' My face was pale with fright and worry. Ratnamma yelled back, 'Shut up! Let me do my job.' Two aides held me down. I could not see what was happening. A quick cut, I assumed, to separate my son from me, and then Ratnamma began to thump him on his back, rather violently, I thought. Suddenly, he started coughing! A welter of emotions, joy, and relief swept through me at that moment. For me, that cough was the most amazing sound on earth.

My son was born on July 2. God had helped me again. It had been a frightening experience, but all was well in the end. I lay down, spent. I could not care less about the blood or the pain. My little son was alive! I was and still am thankful to the Almighty. I called him and still call him the "boy wonder."

The nurses washed my son and brought him to me. All I could see was his hair. My first thought was, *he has so much hair and is so tiny*! I slept, oblivious to my surroundings and the pain. A few hours later, the nurse shook me awake and gave me some food and medicines. The excruciating pain was back. I turned aside to see my son peacefully sleeping. The doctor asked me, 'Is your husband coming? Or anyone else?" She knew my story well since she had been my go-to doctor over the years. She was the one I visited for treatment when Andy beat me. I called my mom's sister, who had a phone and asked her to inform my parents. Andy came late that evening. He was overjoyed. My parents came the next day. My parents-in-law didn't come at all. I felt weak and drained but happy. My son was a tiny bundle of joy. Since he was born with bronchitis, the doctor recommended that I stay in the hospital a little longer. They put him on a strict regimen of antibiotics. He slept peacefully at night.

Andy stayed with me in the hospital. We hadn't named our son, but I instinctively began to call him Sam, simply because I had seen this movie where the little boy's name was Sam. My daughter came with Andy every day. She was thrilled with her baby brother and wanted to take him home immediately to play with him. She thought he was a living doll with whom she could dress and play. *How nice to be little*, I mused.

A few days later, the doctor informed me that Sam was doing well. He was in a stable condition, though he was a little weak and needed extra care. Overall, his health was fine. I authorized my second brother-in-law to collect my salary from my workplace. With that money, I paid the hospital bill, took an autorickshaw, and went back home to Tarnaka.

It was a moment of joy. I had gone to the hospital alone but had returned home with my son in my arms. My parents-in-law seemed pleased to see Sam. This experience was another moment of triumph for me — another validation of the fact that, in spite of the pain and all the other nonsense in my life, I could do anything with Sam and Christina by my side.

My PhD Continues

I had to resume teaching within 21 days after my son was born since I was given notice by the same Principal who was terrorized by Andy that I could lose my job if I did not come back within 20 days. When I came back to work, everyone was stunned at college. I continued and became busy from dawn to dusk. Time never weighed heavily on me; it kept slipping away through my fingers. My parents-in-law took care of my son for a month, after which they said that I should not continue with my education. I became defiant and put him in a daycare. I recall the conditions in the daycare were deplorable, and we had to bring food for the baby. Oftentimes, I felt guilty since I wasn't sure if Sam had his milk, but I continued. My father-in-law doted on Sam, but he could not take care of him alone due to his health. I was called a "bad mother" for studying and wanting a career. People will never understand the heart of a mother at any time. No mother wants bad things for her children. It was like clockwork; I left home at 7.30 am, and Andy or my second brother-in-law dropped my daughter off at school. I dropped my son off at daycare, rushed to Wesley College to teach in the mornings, and rushed to Nizam College at 12.45 pm to continue working towards my PhD program. I left Nizam's at 5 pm, picked up my son from daycare, and came home for a pit stop to go back again to teaching at the tutorials. I was back home by 8 PM.

My daughter had a habit of waiting for me at the gate every evening. When she saw me, her face would light up. Nothing on earth, neither rain nor sun, could stop her from standing there and waiting for me. I looked forward to seeing her stand there and catch her look of joy when she saw me. The fear that she would get wet and catch a cold if it rained made me rush home on time on rainy days. It was only after she became an adult that she told me one day why she had waited like that. 'Ma, I was afraid you wouldn't come back home.' I said, 'Why on earth wouldn't I come home? This is our home!' After staying home for 30 minutes, I would take off on my moped, this time to teach at the tutorial. I coached students preparing for the entrance exam to medical college. My little red moped helped me whizz around without getting too tired.

After dinner, I often studied until late in the night. The birth of my son brought more stability to my life. He was a blessing to me because his birth heralded a new milestone in my personal life — Andy stopped cheating on me. By that time, I was past the pain and anger of being cheated on. Like many 'good' wives, I forgave him. He was the father of my children, after all. It is often said that the woman has to adjust, so I adjusted and compromised with the situation.

Though I still cared for him, I didn't feel the same way about him as I used to earlier. My madness for him was gone. I had become stronger; my goals were tangible and within touching distance.

Dr. Sharon Joshua John

Another Tryst with Destiny

I was quite proud of myself for juggling various responsibilities rather well on a daily basis. I was content with what I had, though I knew that the best was yet to come. I knew Destiny had something wonderful in store for me. I dreamt that I would be traveling the world. The globe would be mine to conquer, and soon, I would be dancing with the wind and the waves, free from the shackles of Hyderabad, which I called 'hell's hole.' God would never fail me; he always keeps his promises. Life continued, and hope prevailed.

One bright afternoon, when I arrived at the university campus, I found two of my classmates smiling and excitedly talking. One of them saw me and exclaimed, 'Great news! Both of us are going to SV University to present at a symposium!' I was surprised. I hadn't heard about any symposium. I asked them for further details. Though I was genuinely happy for them, I was disappointed that I had not been given the same opportunity. If I had been asked to, I would have sent an excerpt of my work to the organizers of the symposium. I could not function well that day; I felt quite low in my spirit.

Three weeks went by uneventfully. Dr. Chary called me into her office and told me that one of my classmates had to drop out of attending the symposium due to personal reasons. She asked me, 'Are you interested in going to SV University to present some of your work? We have a week until the deadline. You will have to work quickly and send in an abstract.' Of course, I said yes. I was thrilled and delighted to have been given a chance! Dr. Chary asked me, 'Are you sure your husband will let you travel out of town?' Without any hesitation, I said, 'Yes, ma'am, this is a brilliant opportunity to present at a global symposium. I will convince him.' She looked at me, rather unconvinced, and said, 'We will see.'

My heart was singing as I went home. I submitted the abstract of my paper the next day and stayed up for a few nights to work on the draft of my presentation. There was a lot of back and forth between my guide and me as we made revision upon revision. We sent the final version of the abstract, and the next two months rolled by as I waited anxiously for the selection.

I received good news and a formal letter of invitation notifying me that I was selected to present at the global symposium at SV University, Tirupati. I sped back home, thrilled to inform Andy about this fantastic opportunity. He did not seem too thrilled about it. His immediate retort was, 'Where will the money for your travel come from? Where will you be staying? What about the children and your job?' On and on his questions went. Disgusted, I asked him, 'Why aren't you happy for me? You always have a problem with whatever I do. Nothing is okay with me in your world. Does it always have to be this way? Ugh!' After a brief pause, I added, 'They aren't giving me any money for travel or accommodation. I have to bear these expenses myself. But this is a once-in-a-lifetime opportunity. I have to go. Also, this is in Tirupati. Don't Hindus consider it a holy place? So why don't we make this a family trip?'

This seemed to quieten him. I was surprised and happy that I seemed to be getting a nod from him. The symposium took place during the summer holidays of schools and colleges, so how would it interfere with my job or the kids' classes? Andy would get free passes to travel by state transport buses since he was working in the state government's road transport corporation.

And so, it was all arranged. I couldn't wait to present my abstract! Andy, too, seemed to be quite enthusiastic because of the free bus tickets. It would be a long, hot journey in the bus, which was a slightly rickety contraption. The windows were open, and the hot sun was beating down. I was happy. Not because of my paper presentation but because the four of us never had a family outing before! The kids enjoyed the ride, especially the climb up the hill. The landscape near Tirupati was breathtaking, and our tired bodies were refreshed as our bus took the winding road. We gazed at the hills, the deep blue sky, and the fluffy white clouds. The air was pure; we breathed in pure oxygen. The rarefied air and the natural beauty of the place quietened even our boisterous kids.

When we arrived in Tirupati, we didn't have time to look for a hotel. I had to sign in at SV University by 9 am, and we were a little rushed. We used the bathrooms at the bus station to have a quick wash. The children bathed under a tap there. Since there was no better place, Andy suggested I change my clothes in one of the empty buses at the bus stand. I did that while he stood guard outside. Even so, by the time we reached the university, it was 9.45 am. I was a little agitated because my presentation was up for 10.30 am. I quickly registered at the reception, where they checked my name and paperwork. Some of the delegates were staring at us since nobody else had come with their family! The people at the reception desk said that registered delegates were allowed into the auditorium. Andy stayed back in the corridor outside with the children.

As I walked into the auditorium, I found that the presentations had begun. The hall seemed to be full. Some people gave me a look as if to say, 'How rude! Couldn't she come on time? This is an international symposium.' One of the ushers said there were vacant seats in the front. I kept my head down and followed him. To my utter consternation, I was escorted to the front row to sit down next to Dr Fingerman, an American professor. I didn't know then that he was one of the judges for the paper presentations! *Breathe, breathe; you made it so far.* I prayed to God and sat down.

When they called out my name, I was jubilant. I presented my work with great enthusiasm and gave prompt responses to the questions from the judges. It was all over in less than 20 minutes! Phew! I came back to my seat and began to chat with the professor. He seemed quite impressed with me. The thrilling moment came after a few minutes. He handed me his business card and asked me if I was interested in coming to the United States after I completed my PhD. If I was, I could contact him. My eyes popped out of their sockets. I could not believe my ears! My heart leapt! I was beyond excited. This was the hand of the Almighty upon me. Fate was about to change my life. I felt jubilant and immediately retorted, 'Yes, I am greatly interested,' and began to converse with the Professor.

My conversation was disturbed when my son came running to me and sat down on my lap. Turning around, I saw Andy and my daughter standing at the back of the auditorium. The next two hours went by peacefully. We broke for lunch. The four of us grabbed some food at the university cafeteria. I waved the business card as if I had won the lottery and shared the good news with Andy. I was not sure what to expect from him. He was thrilled about this development. He was sad that he had had to miss my presentation, he said. I felt like a cloud floating in the skies without a care in the world.

After lunch, the winners of the paper presentation were announced. Another thrilling moment was when I was awarded the prize for the 'best presentation by a promising young researcher.' My son and I trotted up to the stage and received my certificate. I was delirious with delight. My little son did not understand what was happening. He was busy having a great time with the sparkling lights on the stage and refused to get off it. He seemed rather triumphant, standing there as if it were he who had won the prize. Everyone thought this was amusing and cute.

It had been a while since I was this happy. After the awards ceremony, we joined Andy and my daughter. It was a rare moment because all of us were happy. We spent the evening wandering down the streets of Tirupati. We found a cheap hotel to stay in. After spending the next two days in Tirupati and visiting the sanctum sanctorum of the sacred temple, we returned to Hyderabad. Having been on an adrenaline high on the trip, I felt a little tired. I was unutterably happy at having won the prize and, more than that, at having received an invitation of sorts to go to the USA.

Dr. Chary was delighted, too. She was surprised to hear the name of the American professor. She knew Dr. Fingerman from Tulane University in New Orleans, Louisiana, USA, since her Guide worked with him. Small world, indeed! She encouraged me to correspond with Dr. Fingerman and keep in touch with him. Over the next few months, I actively corresponded with Dr. Fingerman.

My Doctorate

I continued with my PhD program. True to his word, Andy stopped cheating on me. I was no longer kicked out of the house to sleep on the veranda outside or walk to my parents' house in the dead of the night. For the first time, I almost felt like I had settled into a happily married life, if such a thing even existed. I was content, for the time being, seeing my American dream take shape. Part of that dream was that Andy would no longer drink and would be a devoted husband and father.

There was an ailment I struggled with on almost a daily basis. I imagined America as a land where my fibromyalgia would vanish and I would experience no pain. I imagined a country where a cure could be found for every ill of the body and the mind. Obviously, I didn't know that the medical insurance system in America is one of the worst in the world. It was perhaps good I didn't know; my ignorance kept my American dream alive and pulsing.

I was diagnosed with fibromyalgia within a year of my wedding. But like most women, I did not understand it, or its full ramifications, initially. As I got older, it took a turn for the worse. It's a strange disease that debilitates me even now, but I have learned to plow through it. I am told it will stay with me for life. Sometimes, it brings me down completely, but at other times, I feel this is not the end. There is so much sickness and disease in this world; this is not the worst of things.

I completed my PhD successfully. My parents were the happiest of my family members. Andy, the kids, and my parents attended my viva voice. My mom said she had never seen me present anything and was extremely proud and impressed with me. Coming from my mother, that was the highest compliment I had ever received. Looking at Mom and Dad, you'd have thought it was *they* who'd earned the PhD. But then, that's true, too. Isn't every victory of a child the victory of their parents, too? My dad never completed high school and started working at a very young age. He felt extremely accomplished that his daughter had achieved this feat and more. Every chance he got, he would boast, 'My daughter is the best. She has always stood first, from KG (kindergarten) to PG (post-graduation)!'

I was offered a full-time job at the prestigious Saint Pious Degree College, which was very close to my home in Tarnaka. My previous job at Wesley had been part-time. That was how I could enroll for PhD while teaching at Wesley. That part-time job, though it didn't pay me much, proved invaluable in freeing my afternoons. I was grateful for that. But now, it was time to step up into a full-time job and earn what I truly deserved.

At St. Pious

I began working as a full-time lecturer at St. Pious. It was an advancement in my career. I felt successful, having achieved my dream of earning a PhD and landing a good job. With an increase in my paycheck, I didn't have to teach at the tutorial institute or coach students for the medical entrance examination. I could return home by 4.30 pm every day. What joy! Spending more time with my children! Life was a bit slower now, after almost six years of college and working part-time. I was able to breathe easier; it was a break from the years of slogging while studying, working, and being a mother, wife, and daughter-in-law in a difficult environment. I was ready, oh so ready, for a life in America.

I was diligent in my correspondence with Dr. Fingerman, with ideas for further research. I kept him abreast of the developments in my academic and professional life. Within a month of my sending him a copy of my PhD certificate, he sent me the documents needed to process my visa to America. I was astonished! It had been so easy! The documents arrived by first-class mail. I didn't have enough money to travel to the States, so it seemed incomprehensible to me that things were moving this fast. Dr. Fingerman's suggestion was that I apply for a post-doctoral fellowship at Tulane University in New Orleans, Louisiana, USA. I thought I could find a job while working on the fellowship.

But for now, I faced a dilemma. At the time of joining Pious as a lecturer, I had had to hand over my original certificates to the college. These would be needed for my visa interview. I spoke to Andy about this. He said, 'Don't worry, it will be the same as in Wesley. If anyone messes with you, I will not be quiet.' I was bemused. This man was ready to kill me for me. At the same time, he could beat me and insult me, too. And in the same breath, say that he loved me. Sigh! To say that he was complicated would not even *begin* to state the truth. I didn't understand him. I didn't understand myself. I simply lived with him and took all the abuse, and yet he had this powerful hold on me.

I said, 'Don't do that! Let me ask the principal first. I'll tell her I can't stay until the end of the academic year since I have to be at Tulane University in the States prior if I get the visa.' Andy said nonchalantly, 'Well, you can try the right way, and then we can do it my way.' I agreed.

The next day, I informed the principal about my plan to go to the USA. 'Ma'am, I have received a wonderful opportunity to go work there. It has been my dream for long. I have to go to the consulate general to get my visa. I need my original certificates for the visa interview.'

I was met with a stony silence. No 'Congratulations!' or 'Oh, that's wonderful!' Instead, the principal said rather curtly, 'Well, it is expected that you continue here until the end of the semester. You can't leave until this academic year has been completed.' She refused to accept my resignation prior to May. My heart sank. I said, 'But ma'am, they expect me to join in January if the visa is approved. It is October now. I am giving a three month notice period. I have completed the entire syllabus for the year. By January, I will have completed any other pending responsibilities, too!'

The principal asked me to come back the next day. She said she wanted to speak to the head of the department. I left rather disheartened. When I returned home that evening, I found my dad visiting us. Andy hadn't gone to work that day since we were getting ready to travel to Bombay for the visa interview. When I told both of them what transpired in the principal's office, they were tense. I had all the required documents except for the certificates. Andy said, 'Oh well, I knew it. It's time to take action.' I said, 'Andy, no. I don't want another altercation in college. I need to keep this job until I leave for the States because I still haven't gotten the visa!' But Andy was Andy. He was adamant, saying, 'We will get the certificates and the money, *and* you will get the visa. Everything will happen in time.' I had to give in.

The next day, he came with me to meet the principal. It was a miracle that he did not say much to her, but his presence alone was probably enough to intimidate her. Magically, her behavior that day was completely different. She congratulated us and said that my certificates would be handed over, but I would have to stay on my job until at least the first week of January.

'Of course, ma'am, of course!' I said, beaming.

Visa to America

I had the certificates and other documents required for the visa application. But where was the money? My dad had received some money from selling his ancestral property in Maredpally, another suburb of Hyderabad. This house had been lovingly built by my Nainamma and my grandpa. My dad had not given me a share of the money, not that I cared, saying Andy might waste it. Everything had gone to my brother and his family. My brother had sold his inheritance and lost the rest of the money in a business that never took off.

I asked my parents to help me. I was in dire need, I said. I would return the money to them when I started earning. I knew my parents were not wealthy. They had to keep something for their old age. So, being a conscientious child, I was clear that I would repay this money soon.

But, to my dismay, my parents told me that the money had been spent and was no longer available! Tears rolled down my cheeks. My parents had promised me that they would finance my trip to the USA with some of this money!

I was happy that Andy was extremely supportive at such a time and did not fly off the handle as usual. On the contrary, he was very proud that I had received admission to Tulane University as a post-doctoral research fellow. We decided to keep this a secret from the family until I got my visa and bought my tickets.

Many people whom we know in the family had gone to the USA on a six-month religious visa, overstayed, became illegal, worked the system to their benefit, and have currently become citizens after decades. Immigration is still a problem in the United States. Others had gotten 'visas through marriage.' I was truly the first person in my family at that time to come to the United States on a J-1 Postdoctoral fellowship. Some of the people in my family who had applied for a US visa had been rejected several times and had immigrated to other countries. America, the great nation! I had fallen in love with it even without seeing it. To me, it was certainly the land of milk and honey. To live there was an honor and prestige bestowed on a few people, I thought. I felt chosen by the Almighty himself. He had not left me. He was always by my side, helping me in times of trouble. My dad was extremely proud of me and often bragged among the family, much to the ire of others, stating, "America needs her! This is why they have called her." He also sometimes poked fun at them, stating, 'My daughter did not do anything illegal.'

Andy's excitement was contagious. Curiously, I felt more connected to him now than ever before. Perhaps this connection was fleeting, but I didn't think much about it. I knew he loved me in his peculiar way and would follow me to the ends of the earth.

After several anxious days of wondering how to raise the money, Mom said to me, 'Baby, I have a piece of land that I have bought. We could mortgage this piece of land, but you have to pay this money back to the bank since it is still being paid off monthly.' Desperate to grab any ray of sunshine, I replied immediately, 'Yes, of course, Mom. I will pay the bank once I am in the States and take up the monthly payments.' Mom cautioned me again that I had to pay the money back *on time* lest my parents should lose the land. Again, I promised her that I would send her money every month.

We went to the bank. Sadly, they offered us limited funding; it would not be enough for my trip and a few months of expenses in the USA. I later discovered that my Nainamma had willed some of the Maredpally property to me besides my brother. My parents never shared this fact with me. In her will, which was not registered, Nainamma had bequeathed the Marredpally plot and house to Dad since he wasn't as well-off as his siblings. All his siblings were educated and had good, stable jobs. My dad had helped his mom, my Nainamma by cooking for his siblings, packing their lunches, taking care of his younger sisters, cleaning, and later, financially, when he began working. Nainamma's will stated that the property should remain with Dad and his children and should not be sold.

Years later, sometime in 2017, I saw this will, which is now in my possession, while I was rummaging through the documents after my dad passed away. It had not been executed according to her wishes. It made me terribly sad. But I also understood by that time that I had achieved a lot in life. It dawned on me that my Nainamma's blessings had been with me all along and that I had inherited more wealth, respect, love, and blessings from my immediate family. I was truly grateful. It was those blessings and the Hand of the Almighty that brought me to America so that I could help my parents in their old age, my brother and his family in their days of illness until they all sadly passed away.

Filled with anxiety, joy, and fear of the unknown, I left Hyderabad for Bombay to visit the American consulate and appear for the visa interview. My dad and Andy accompanied me. We reached Bombay a day ahead. People were allowed into the consulate on a first-come-first-served basis, and they started forming a queue the previous night itself! No one was allowed to enter the premises without valid documents.

The next day, we joined this queue. I wore my mother's chocolate brown saree and neatly braided my hair. My glasses made me look rather studious — the typical post-doctoral research fellow. Andy and my dad said they would wait outside the premises, though I said it could be hours before I was called for my interview.

We prayed while standing on the street, and I went inside, rather stressed after rehearsing all the questions that could be potentially asked of me. Those of us waiting for the interview were asked to wait in an anteroom of sorts. One by one, we were called and asked to hand over the relevant documents at the counter. My package of documents contained my bank account statement, marriage certificate, birth certificate, academic certificates, and other details, which were organized as per the given instructions. The man at the counter looked at me quizzically and said that nothing was required except for my IAP-66, which was a one-page document sent by Tulane University and my passport. Puzzled, I handed these over to him; he gave me a receipt with a number. He then told me to wait. Everyone had warned us that the process could take hours and sometimes, the consulate general grilled the applicant with questions. My mind was spinning with a million thoughts as I waited.

Fifteen minutes later, they called out a number. I wasn't paying attention since I was busy rehearsing the questions and responses in my mind. They called out the number again, and I realized with a start that it was my turn! I got up and walked to a different counter. I paid the visa fee, as instructed by the man sitting there. I asked him, 'Will I be interviewed right now?' He replied, 'There is no interview. You have gotten your visa already.' I stared at him in disbelief. I then said to him incredulously, 'But sir, I am confused. No interview?' He repeated, 'No, there is no need for an interview.'

Speechless and jubilant, I collected the fee receipt. The man then said, 'Come by 4 pm to collect your passport, stamped with the American visa.' After asking him another time if there was to be no interview and receiving the same reply as before from him, I skipped out of the campus. I thought Andy and Dad would have left for the hotel to return after a few hours, but they were standing outside. My dad was puzzled and a tad worried. He came rushing to me and asked me, 'What happened? Did they ask you for other documents?' Andy, too, could not understand why I had left the consulate within less than 30 minutes. I told them to calm down and explained what had happened. Their look of worry turned to one of exultation as they heard me. 'A visa without an interview! I've never seen anything like this!' my dad exclaimed. We realized that it was called a counter visa. It was a rare occasion when I saw my dad weep, tears of happiness, of course. Excitedly, we left, grabbed a sumptuous lunch and came back to collect the stamped passport at 4 pm.

Back in Hyderabad, I started preparing earnestly for my journey. It was October of 1997. My fellowship began on Jan 23, 1998. *Hardly any time to get ready for my trip,* I thought. It hit me that I would be going alone. I was terrified of leaving the kids but consoled myself, saying I would call them and Andy over soon and that we would do well in the States.

I bought five pairs of clothes and two pairs of shoes. That was a big deal for me! I had never bought so many new clothes since I was married. Trousers, shirts, suits…I felt like a princess. Everything was rushed. I was afraid to leave my children in Andy's care. I was sure he and his friends would be partying day in and day out, knowing I wasn't there. Andy said he would not do that, but I had my doubts. I told him I'd leave the children with my parents until Andy and the children joined me in the States. He agreed. It was a tough situation; I hadn't realized so many arrangements had to be made!

Finally, everything was done.

Amidst much kissing, hugging, smiling, and crying, I boarded the flight to America. Andy looked worried. He told me not to forget him. *Funny*, I thought. Dad's parting words to me were, 'Even if I die, don't come back, baby. You will be successful there.' My son was too little to understand what was happening; my daughter was sad. Mom, as usual, was calm and happy.

It was my first time on a flight! Such fun! The feeling was indescribable. I settled into my seat and looked out the window. It seemed incredulous to understand that my dream was coming true. I was looking forward to the next chapter of my life.

On Jan 13, 1998, I landed in New Orleans, USA.

A Post-Doc Fellow at Tulane

New Orleans was nothing like I had imagined it to be! The streets were clean and rather empty. I was to meet Professor Fingerman at 10 am on the day of my arrival. I took a taxi from the airport directly to Tulane University. I reached the University Center with two suitcases and waited. Professor Fingerman was in class, they said. I had to wait a good two hours to meet him. He was happy to see me and congratulated me on making it to the USA. We exchanged notes on what needed to be done in the next few days. By that time, I was exhausted. I needed to crash somewhere soon. I checked into a hotel near the campus. The room rate was a bit much, but what could I do? There was no other hotel in that area. I was scared, lonely and sad. I had landed in the USA with 800 dollars. I consoled myself, saying in a few days, I would shift to a room on the university campus with the professor's help. I understood from University Services that an apartment within the campus was 500 dollars without a deposit. Hearing this, I panicked! That was more than half the money I had!

I began discussing my program in detail with Prof. Fingerman. I familiarized myself with the topic he had outlined for me. I was excited to join the program. My financial situation was concerning. While I had paid the rent for my apartment for the first month, I couldn't survive the second month if I didn't make further arrangements. I did what I could to skimp on expenses, like eating once a day or once in two days. I talked to some people about finding a job. I was distraught and missed my home and my family.

My professor expressed his displeasure about my financial situation. He said he expected me to sustain myself for several months, at the least when I shared my concerns with him. 'Most students came adequately prepared,' he said. I did not know what to say. Call it my naivete or whatever; I was learning many fundamental things about the program and about life in New Orleans only after landing in the States. I learned that I would not be paid for the program; the professor said he hadn't received the funds he had been expecting from the National Health Institute (NIH). I approached the University International Service Center and met the International admissions counselor. I asked her how I could support myself financially. She said I could enquire at the Dean's office; they might have some openings to work on campus. I had thought America was a land of milk and honey, where there was no lack of anything.

A few other students from India taught me about immigration laws, which were tough. It was impossible to work outside the university, though some did dare to do this on the sly. I was afraid to break the law or do anything else that would jeopardize my situation. I made brief phone calls to India but could not talk much; I was afraid of wasting money on calls. I took to writing letters. I did not write about any of my difficulties.

Thankfully, I found a job at the Dean's office, since I could work on-campus. It was an administrative job. Not fancy, I know, but it was a job. It would pay me at least *something*, I reasoned. I started going to the university at 7 am to work and carry out research for my fellowship. I worked on weekends, too.

On one of my calls to India, I told my parents that it'd be tough for me to pay back the loan I had taken from them by mortgaging their property. I asked if I could postpone the payments. Mom said, 'Baby, come back to India. Your husband has taken the children back to his house. We cannot go and stay there. God knows what their plight is.' I was shocked. I said, 'Mom, no, I cannot come back. As it is, I am in a difficult situation. Coming back will make it worse. I am not sure what I can do about this. Let me talk to Andy.' Dad chimed in and immediately said, 'No, don't come back. We can manage. Maybe I will go and stay with the children.' I had to strike an unhappy truce with our situation and felt rather distressed.

Other students told me I could apply for another fellowship since I was in, and under the J1 visa program, it would be easier. I would then be paid a stipend. Back in Hyderabad, Andy continued drinking as usual. My parents and I were worried about the effect this would have on the children. It was becoming increasingly difficult for me not to do anything. Whenever I spoke to Andy, he said, 'Oh, it looks like you won't come back and you're going to forget me.' I wished he would not say such things, but well…

The university counselor informed me that one could bring one's spouse to the USA on a J2 visa, which was rather easy, and that they could work legally in New Orleans! I thought this was a great opportunity for Andy to come, provided he funded his trip himself. I was excited at this prospect since the children could live with my parents.

In a month, I was able to send Andy the required documentation for his trip to the United States. Expectedly, he was jubilant. We had never imagined that I'd be able to do this so soon! I, too, was thrilled since I missed him terribly. Next, it would be the turn of the kids, I promised myself.

Andy Joins Me

Andy had to raise the money for his ticket to the States. He borrowed it from his father and signed a few documents that I have no idea about, even up till today. He was ready to sign away his life to join me, I heard from my parents. I had told him that he had to bring at least 800 dollars. He could then find work here and start earning immediately. The immigration laws were so strange; the J1 visa holder could work 20 hours per week on campus, whereas the J2 dependent visa holder could work 40 hours outside campus. Oh well!

I arrived in January, and Andy came to the United States in March of the same year. He was unrecognizable. He had lost a lot of weight and looked fatigued. As soon as he saw me, he fell into my arms and started crying. It shocked me that he had missed me so much; I wept, too. The next few days were like a honeymoon for us. It seemed like a dream. Our excitement for our future was palpable. We were all set to begin a new life together. Andy said, 'This is all great, but I am missing the hustle-bustle of Hyderabad. It is lonely here — no neighbors, not many people around! No friends, haha!' I thought this would teach him a lesson not to drink excessively and guffawed at him.

I had to agree with him. 'But who cares, Andy? We are here to stay and become famous!' I said. He smiled and looked at me as if I were his new bride. I felt special. We spent the first few days chatting about Hyderabad, our kids, how they missed us, our parents, our friends, and our dreams. We would talk till the wee hours of the morning and yet not feel tired. I took Andy to the International Students Center on the university campus to find out about getting a work permit and a job for him. He seemed surprised that I did not venture outside the campus much. But to me, the campus had become home. It had everything I needed; I was self-sufficient here. I told Andy about the living expenses. Fortunately, we had sufficient money to pay the rent for my fourth month there.

We were in for a rude awakening when we came to know that Andy's work permit would take a minimum of 90 days and that we had to pay 120 dollars for it! That would leave us with a month's rent. We had to move into a room-share to reduce our rental expenses. *Ninety days without a work permit*, I thought. We felt gloomy.

In an effort to cheer ourselves up a bit, we got out of the confines of our room on weekends and walked miles on end, aimlessly. Though we were a bit sad, our spirits were up about how things would get better soon. The fact that our children were safe and comfortable with my parents also helped boost my morale.

We ate once in three days. I shudder to think of it. I have no clue how we managed that, but then, I was used to eating sparingly, even back in India, when I was preoccupied with my studies, job, and other problems.

The house we moved into was shared with us by six other students. Engrossed in my research and job, I didn't notice time fly. Andy's work permit arrived, and he found a job at an Exxon gas station nearby. He was very proud of himself. He had walked miles during the previous days, looking for work. He got this job at the gas station by chance. A man named Mr. Ali from India owned the Exxon gas station on South Claiborne. Andy's charming nature could captivate people's hearts. He talked to Mr. Ali and, within an hour, got himself hired. I was very proud of him.

Andy told me he had stopped drinking five months ago. He was a reformed man, he claimed. It was another matter that he soon resumed the habit. 'Just a beer, now and then,' he told me. And soon, he began to slip back into his old ways. Still, I was happy to be without the strains of living in a joint family and facing interference from friends. Andy could live anywhere; he was adaptable and charismatic and could make friends easily. Though he missed his drinking binges with his old friends, he began to make new ones at the gas station. Another thing I was grateful for was that he wasn't beating me as much as before. Oh, yes! The abuse and the beatings did start, in case you were wondering. I found it strange that I kept justifying everything he did by convincing myself one way or another. I didn't understand it then. I stopped trying to figure out things and was more focused on my goals of bettering our lives for the sake of the children.

I consider myself intelligent, resilient, resourceful, and persevering. These qualities and hope kept me alive and moving ahead all the time. I definitely wasn't a victim of circumstances but a *child* of circumstances. I made the best of every situation, good or bad, and managed to turn my dreams into reality. I prayed that I would bring my children to the USA the same year. Much would depend upon the Almighty, who had shone His grace upon me all along.

 I was impatient to see my children. I couldn't call them on the phone as often as I wanted to. If only I could earn more money! That's when the idea suggested by the counselor at the International Students Center started taking root in my mind, and I decided to apply to another university for a post-doctoral fellowship that paid a stipend. I felt hopeful that I would find such a position soon enough.

Post-Doc Fellow At Ochsner

It was exhausting; I completed my work in the lab and worked for a few hours at the Dean's office, and the entire day was gone. After that, I went to the library to browse the local newspapers for jobs and surf the internet. The web was a totally new world to me. Browsing the web was expensive in India, and I had never done it there. Here, it was easy and free within the campus. What's more, I was thrilled that my typing skills were coming in handy! Who knew that the hateful *clack clack clack* I detested at the typewriting institute in Hyderabad would help me one day in a new way? Being no expert, I typed rather slowly.

I began to apply for jobs. I thought of my mom and thanked her for sending me to the best schools. That helped me become extremely organized and systematic in my approach.

The money Andy and I had was sufficient for rent and groceries for a little while. I could not yet repay the loan I had taken from my parents. I received one on-site interview at Ochsner Hospital in New Orleans. This was the biggest Health Maintenance Organization (HMO) in the state of Louisiana. We took a bus ride to see how the location of the hospital. Both of us were shocked to see the size of this hospital. We stood there, gaping at the several tall buildings on the hospital campus that seemed to sprawl over miles and miles. I was nervous and excited about the interview and studied avidly for the same.

I did the interview well, although anxiety followed later. Two days later, I received a phone call informing me that I had got the job! That's it, just a phone call!

I was instructed to proceed to the Human Resources department and complete the relevant paperwork. It was a process that took an hour or two. Thus began a memorable and wonderful 6-year chapter of my career. The people at Ochsner were kind and warm. I had wonderful colleagues and was able to transfer my post-doctoral fellowship from Tulane University to Ochsner Hospital. It was a triumphant moment. Though I'd initially be paid a stipend there, it still was a lot of money for me! I felt like an empress rolling in wealth and splendor.

In July of 1998, I was able to think of bringing our children to the United States. Things were moving in the right direction, considering my initial difficulties in this land of plenty. My career would never have progressed this rapidly if I had remained in India. Bringing my husband over in three months after I landed in the United States, landing a paid post-doctoral research fellowship in one of the largest HMOs in the United States in another seven months, thinking of bringing my children to join us within a year — what more could I want! I was living the American dream, where hard work pays off. Indeed, the Hand of God was upon me yet again. The future looked bright; there was a lot we could build on in the USA. I was thrilled, and so was Andy.

Since our children were minors, they would not be able to travel alone. Andy said, "Let's ask my manager to sponsor your dad to the United States. Your dad can accompany the kids." I was afraid to ask his manager, but Andy was all about being bold and asking for things. He used to say, 'If you don't ask, you won't receive'. He worked the afternoon shift and came back home late at night. That night, I waited for him anxiously to return, wondering what news he'd come bearing. Hearing his knock on the door, I opened it with bated breath. I said two words to him, but those two words held all the nervousness, anxiety, and hope I was feeling. 'What happened?'

He looked at me for a moment as if to draw out the suspense and said excitedly, 'Yes, yes, yes! I told you Mr. Ali is a good man. When I told him our children couldn't travel alone, he immediately agreed to send your dad visitor visa sponsorship documents.' Thrilled, I immediately called my parents and informed them of this exciting news. I added that we would soon send my dad documents for his travel. Oh, how I missed my children! I could only sponsor my children.

I had already begun to find out about travel itineraries and the education system in the USA. I sent my parents a list of the vaccinations the kids would need to take. Birth certificates, passports, vaccination cards, and work had to be in order. I was dancing around like a child!

The tiny studio apartment Andy and I were living in would not be sufficient for all of us. We thought we would move to a bigger apartment when the kids and my dad arrived. We began to visit downtown New Orleans during the weekends. We'd have a lazy time, simply walking around and watching people while eating street food called jambalaya and gobbling sugary beignets at Café Du Monde. We also liked to visit the riverwalk and gaze at the mighty Mississippi River. I was so much at peace.

Soon, we moved into a two-bedroom apartment less than a mile from Ochsner Hospital and began to buy furniture and other stuff for our new home. We rummaged through thrift stores, where used goods were sold at low prices, and were able to get tables, a couch, and a few chairs. It was amazing how helpful people could be and how little we had to spend on furniture at thrift stores. We barely had any money, and yet, we had the world at our feet. The heavens seemed to have opened up to shower their blessings upon us.

We started preparing the home for my dad and the kids.

Dr. Sharon Joshua John

My Children are in the USA

I had come to the United States on Jan 13, 1998. Andy had arrived on March 8, 1999. My children and my dad arrived on November 23, 1999. I was able to send the required visa documents for Andy and my children. Mr. Ali sent the required documents for my dad since I was still on a J-1 visa and could not sponsor my parents. I financed my children's and my dad's trip. It surprised and delighted me that I was doing something nobody else in my family had done. The surprise has given way to a growing astonishment over the years as I look back at those times. Even today, some of my family members haven't received their green cards and are unable to sponsor their children or spouses. Surely, God had blessed us abundantly.

My kids and my dad landed in New Orleans. We brought them home from the airport by bus since we could not afford a taxi and had no car. My dad's excitement mirrored that of the children; it was his first time in the United States. The kids were excited, not about landing in the United States but about being with Andy and me. We stayed up all night, talking and catching up on every little thing in our lives. I was amazed at how tall my son had grown! Or was the mom in me imagining it? My daughter looked content and happy. None of us were tired.

Andy and I took the next day off from work. After a few hours of sleep, we visited downtown. My dad and the kids were fascinated by the riverwalk. Within a few days, the kids were admitted to school; I had initiated the paperwork prior to their arrival to the States, so this didn't take much time. The same month, my dad got a job at a gas station through a friend of mine. However, in a few days, he told us he couldn't continue working there as he had never worked at a cash register and felt uncomfortable with it. Angry, I told him off. 'Dad, we can't choose in this country. We all have a hard life, at least for some time. We have to adjust to whatever we get! This is how all immigrants begin life here.'

I continued, 'I have a PhD and worked as a lecturer in a college in India. But here, I was conducting pre-clinical research, cleaning the cages of animals. I even worked in a dean's office, filing documents! This is how it is for most post-doctoral fellows here. Whatever your field of work, you adjust and grow from there.'

Anyway, after my spiel, Andy spoke to Mr. Ali again and tried to get my dad a job at Mr. Ali's brother's store. That, too, didn't work out. Andy and I were frustrated, but we didn't give up hope. Meanwhile, my dad helped us with the kids, getting them ready in the morning, taking them to school, and bringing them back later in the day. My daughter took a while to adjust to the new environment in school, but my son seemed to take to it like fish to water. He adjusted well and made several friends at the apartment complex.

Overall, life was fun and peaceful, although Andy was drinking daily. I asked him to tone it down but to no avail. Sometimes, we argued about it; sometimes, I kept quiet. However, a good thing about moving to the United States was that he did not beat me as much as before. What a relief! You may be amazed that I was taking it with such composure. Do you see it as a sign of my weakness? I know; it seems inexplicable even to me. But, as I said earlier, I was never able to decipher fully the way my relationship with Andy worked — what truly made it tick, what made me take all the abuse I took from him and yet stay with him. No woman should be physically or verbally abused. So why didn't I complain to the authorities about Andy or walk out on him? It was all so tangled in a sense, so the best way, I have learned, is to accept whatever happened and not judge myself as what I could have or could not have done.

I could tolerate Andy's verbal abuse and daily drinking better than his physical abuse. I kept imagining that he would somehow stop drinking every day and drink socially and stop abusing me. He did stop philandering after the birth of our son, and curiously, our being in the United States made his beating more bearable. Incredulous statement! I think at this point in my life. Perhaps this was because my career was steadily improving, and with that, my confidence was soaring. I wasn't trapped in a dark hole anymore; I had taken flight.

Sometimes, I wonder if I made the right decision by calling my dad over to the United States. He then invited his elder brother, who lived in Hawaii without our permission, to visit us. This caused Andy and me a lot of aggravation. My dad's elder brother was judgmental of Andy's drinking and kept harassing me and the kids to call the cops.

I spoke sternly to my dad again. 'Dad, first off, this is *our* home; you should have asked me before calling your brother over. Also, the apartment management will not appreciate so many people living in a two-bedroom apartment since we did not sign up for so many. In fact, they could consider this illegal! And finally, he is aggravating Andy. I cannot stop Andy's drinking, but at least things are better here than in India! I cannot expect Andy to magically change; this is a process, but it's much better now. Ask your brother to leave, or I shall.' I had just filed my I-140 for the green card. I told Dad I could not jeopardize the immigration process under any circumstance; we could not be in trouble with the law for not our fault.

My dad and his elder brother shared an uneasy relationship, with a history of arguing and fighting over several issues since their childhood. It seemed that age hadn't mellowed them; they often got into boisterous, fiery arguments. This was totally unpleasant, and it made me think of Hyderabad all over again. I feared that if my uncle continued to stay with us, there could be trouble for all of us.

And it did! I got a call from the apartment association's office, saying our neighbors were complaining about noise from my apartment and that the cops would be called if this continued. I went home and asked my uncle to leave that very day. Though this was probably rather unceremonious, I felt compelled to do this since I had to protect my family. That week was a harrowing experience that left Andy angry. His anger seeped into the next week. My uncle's aggravating presence had set off the fuse in him. I, too, argued with my dad; overall, it wasn't a pleasant experience for any of us. I didn't know then that the acrimonious episodes of that week would cast a long shadow on our family life.

Some things cannot be forgotten; they change one's destiny forever. In spite of myself, I have wondered several times over the years: 'What might have happened if this had not happened?' Often, I don't have a clear answer. *What might have happened* is in the world of speculation.

Though hard, I have learned that one can smile away pain and think of the good memories left behind by loved ones. Our power to forgive is great and vital for our mental peace in the little time we have on earth. Coming across palpable hate and strife across the face of the earth, including in families, I wonder if people think they will live forever. In the 21st century, technology and social media, although informative, have also sown the seeds of strife and turmoil. At the end of the day, relationships are all that matter, and an act of kindness goes a long way.

Dr. Sharon Joshua John

Trouble With The Law

My uncle's visit left an uneasy feeling at home in its wake. Isn't it said that 'better is a dry morsel with quietness than a house full of feasting with strife'? Wise words, indeed. In India, we believe that when some people step into your home, chaos ensues. Being a researcher at heart, I do not believe in superstition. But sometimes, I wonder when things that science cannot explain happen. Is that the will of the Almighty? The mystical thing people call destiny? I know not. Some things can never be explained.

Oh, such a blessing to be a kid! Our kids escaped the tension at home by running around the apartment building and playing with their friends — in spite of the cold. A fun part of living in Deckbar Apartments was that our children had plenty of friends and could safely play inside the apartment complex itself.

My uncle began calling the kids on the phone every day when Andy and I were not at home; when my kids returned home from school at 3 pm, we came home later during the evening. He would tell my daughter, 'Call the cops on your father. This country does not put up with domestic violence. I wonder why your mother is tolerating this behavior. You children are being affected by it.' My daughter told me about these calls after a few days. I went berserk, blocking my uncle's number and confronting my dad again. 'Why did you invite this man into my home? He has enraged my husband and me and is filling my daughters' ears with nonsense. Is this right?' Not that what my uncle had said about Andy's behavior was wrong. But he had no right to interfere in my family's matters! And if he wanted to talk about it, I thought he should do so with *me*, not my kids!

My dad seemed unperturbed. He thought it could be a good thing to call the cops. This inflamed me further. Andy was angry, too. He did what he usually did when angry and that was to drink excessively. That weekend, he drank more than usual and was unusually quiet. I felt the rumblings of fear in my stomach but somehow quelled them and stayed silent. They proved to be prophetic. The old enmity between my dad and Andy soon reared its ugly head.

With tempers already running high, the spark that had been lit the previous week by the episode involving my uncle was about to explode. Andy and I got into an argument, as usual, and he began beating me. Oh! All hell broke loose when he started slapping me around. I fought back more fiercely than usual, which resulted in more beatings.

My son ran out of the apartment. My dad took my daughter to another room and shut the door. Everything was a blur for me as I hit the floor. It had been quite some time since I had been beaten like this. The next thing I knew, the cops arrived.

The ominous way a cop knocks on the door and how he barges in wasn't something I had expected to see in real life. It shook me to the core. For many days afterward, I had nightmares of cops barging into our house and arresting Andy. In fact, the sound of their knocks reverberates in my ears even today. It affected me so much that I stopped watching crime shows on TV for several years.

The cops arrested Andy. It was a terrible sight to behold; he was handcuffed and made to lie on the floor while they searched the house and demanded to know if he had a weapon. They took photos of my bruised face and body. It was terribly humiliating! I began crying, pleading with them to let him go, but to no avail. I feared for Andy's safety and life. To my disbelief, Andy himself seemed calm and unruffled. I felt a million emotions passing through my mind as he stood there and told me, 'Don't worry, Sharon. I will be back.' Was he mad, or was I? It was all over in less than 20 minutes. The kids were obviously upset at seeing their dad being taken away. Try as I might, I could not console either them or myself. It was past 2 am. Beside myself with worry and grief, I waited for the morning so I could talk to Mr. Ali, Andy's manager.

The nightmare that began that day continued for the next three years or so. My immigration process was heavily delayed because I refused to go ahead with the next step, i.e., the I-485, which was the second step of the immigration process, without Andy's name on the application. I was the primary applicant. The lawyer said I could file for the second step of immigration with the kids, dropping Andy's name without his knowledge. He said I could add his name after my immigration had been cleared. I refused, since I wasnt sure if Andy's name could be added later. What if he did not qualify for immigration later and had to be left out completely?

In a tragic twist of fate, my long wait to have Andy's name cleared by the cops and added to the immigration application proved to be of no avail. Our green cards arrived in May of 2003, three months later after Andy had tragically passed away in February of 2003. I gazed at his green card for almost an hour, thinking of what he used to say, 'I will get the green card and visit India. I'll meet all my friends and come back.' Maybe that hope had kept him going; I am not sure.

I have made peace with his death. Every human being arrives in this world, and the time and date of their death are stamped on their destiny. Death is part of the natural course of life. Still, I wish Andy had lived longer and enjoyed life in the USA with the kids and me for some more time. At least, he would have left this world after enjoying his green card status for a while. Who knows! This question nags me even today.

Anyway, let me get back to his arrest. At around 7 am, Andy called me from the jail he was housed in. He said, 'Sharon, can you get me released? I promise I will never beat you again.' I started crying and said, 'I am so sorry this is happening to us. I am going to meet Mr. Ali immediately. I don't know anyone else who can help us.' Sending the children off to school, I went to the gas station where Andy worked. It was with great shame that I told Mr. Ali about the situation we were in. He was shocked yet calm and composed. Since he could not leave the gas station just then, he asked me to wait awhile. He said he would contact his elder brother to find out how to post bail. I felt sorry for him, seeing his confusion. It was an unusual situation for him, he said, since he had never visited a police station or jail in the 30-odd years he had been in the United States. I hoped he and his brother would be able to post bail.

I had to be at work by 8.30 am. I thanked Mr. Ali and left rather anxiously, leaving my heart at the gas station. Wasn't that what I always did — compartmentalize my work and my personal life so that one did not interfere with the other? All this was a bit much, even for me, less than two years of coming to America. And to think this happened within three months of my dad's arrival.

The Mayhem Continues

It was almost 9 pm the next day by the time bail was posted for Andy. I was worried sick since I did not have any money. Everything was done by Mr. Ali. Andy refused to talk about anything that had happened in the jail and never mentioned the night he spent there. It was awful. We came home, spent. I refused to talk to my dad and could not even bring myself to look at him. I did not understand myself and was disgusted about the entire situation. I had come to America to rid our family of cops, but they were back in my home again! This was not how I wanted to live in the United States.

The next step of my immigration, which was the application of the I-485, was going to be a nightmare. With a heavy heart, I informed the lawyer that my husband had been arrested and this could pose a problem with the immigration authorities. He agreed, saying it was potentially devastating; Andy now had a 'record.' We would need to wait for a while to apply for the I-485 processing.

While we were going through this turbulence, familial issues and arguments resumed back in India. As usual, my brother and his wife had misunderstandings with my mom. My mom asked my dad to come back to India. It hadn't been even six months, and she was already asking my dad to return! Was this déjà vu? I recall that my mom had asked me to come back to India within three weeks of my landing in New Orleans. I begged her not to ask my dad to return to India. But he, too, was adamant that he had to go back. I pleaded with my mom to stay with her sister for some time, which she did. I thought my dad should stay in the USA, get a better job, and bring Mom over, too! All of us could be together in the USA. Since my dad did not have any formal education, I was trying to get him admission into a community college to train to become a chef; this way, he could immigrate to the United States and help my mom and brother and his family. My children and Andy were on a J2 visa and were eligible to work legally in the USA. Since I did not have a green card, I could not sponsor my parents. Andy and I were thinking of different ways for the betterment of the family. Our intentions and efforts were futile since my dad chose to do what he wanted.

My dad was adamant that he wanted to return to India. After all the chaos he and his brother had created. Andy and I would now be shouldering another big financial burden since I would have to borrow money to pay for my dad's ticket. Gifts for the family had to be bought. This is a huge expectation when anyone goes back to India.

I thought the matter of Andy's arrest was over. But I forgot that this was America. In the USA, domestic violence is dealt with strictly and swiftly. Also, we were immigrants, so the matter was viewed more seriously. Lawyers, courts, and cops plagued us for the next three years, with far-reaching repercussions and grief for both me and Andy.

I received a letter from the authorities asking me to attend court and testify against Andy. Shock and rage filled me; I did not understand this! I thought this was crazy. How was this possible? I had not pressed charges against Andy! I had not called the cops. I had not complained to anyone! I broke down, feeling helpless and cheated by life again. I thought I would never be given a chance to lead a happy married life. It had been nothing but turbulent from the day I left home to get married.

Even in those depths of despair, I somehow found the strength to go on. I consulted another lawyer, which, of course, involved spending more of the money we did not have. Thankfully, I was on a payment plan with the lawyer. This lawyer was able to work out a deal for Andy to join a pre-trial diversion program, which included 'batterer intervention counseling.' Andy had to attend the program diligently and not skip any counseling sessions. Or he would go onto trial. He had to attend classes twice a month for six months. I accompanied him, but they did not allow me to attend the class with him. Andy began to argue with the counselor, saying, 'In India, slapping your wife is not a big issue. Later, the husband and wife become one again. The matter is forgotten, and we forgive each other.' I couldn't understand his nonchalance. Andy did not understand the gravity of his situation!

Predictably, he was thrown out of the program, and the case went to trial. We hired the same lawyer; the trial dragged on for two years. It was in April 2002 that Andy was finally cleared, and the case closed. *Yes*! What a relief! The next week itself, after what seemed to be an eternity, I applied for the I-485, the second step of the immigration process. Andy jumped for joy when I did this, exulting, 'I will get the green card, go to India, tell everyone about it, and come back.' He said this to whoever he spoke to. He was like that, my Andy — childlike at times.

His drinking did not stop, but at least his beatings did. Yes, they stopped. Andy told me that, in the USA, men who were jailed for beating their women were severely beaten up by the other prisoners. Whereas the prisoners apparently respected someone who'd been jailed for murder! I didn't know whether to believe him or not. I was enormously relieved that he stopped beating me; my body had been battered enough. How strange it felt — such a relief after years of suffering his abuse! I was happy and grateful.

Dr. Sharon Joshua John

The Diagnosis

We tried to do a lot over the weekends as a family, often going to parks, downtown New Orleans, St Charles Street, the riverwalk, taking the ferry, and so on. Such fun! For those few years, it was the four of us; it was wonderful, in spite of the sadness. Though anxious about our future, we managed to live in the day and find moments to cherish. You could do so many things in New Orleans without spending much — or any — money. When Andy drank excessively and could not make it to our weekend outings, the kids and I spent time on the banks of the Mississippi. My son skated, and my daughter jogged with me. Those were some of our happiest times in spite of Andy's everyday drinking. Life wasn't so bad, after all. *I could settle into this kind of life*, I thought.

We loved taking pictures. I, especially, tried to capture every good moment. So much so that after he grew up, my son was able to put together an album of more than 500 pictures that had the four of us together! If only those times had lasted longer! But our lives soon took a drastic turn, and another insurmountable difficulty reared its ugly head on our path.

Andy began to gain weight around his midriff. I made fun of him at times, although he did not seem to mind it. After a few months, his legs began to swell enormously. I could not understand it, but he attributed it to his standing for 8 hours every day while working at the Exxon gas station. I told him to take breaks, which he said he did. He complained of pain in his legs almost every day. He seemed sluggish, too, and did not want to do much during the weekends. His health became rather worrisome, and his weight gain was rather strange. I carted him off to the doctor, though he protested the entire time.

The doctor ran some tests. The diagnosis was alarming: cirrhosis of the liver. At first, I did not realize the seriousness of the situation and could not believe this was happening. Andy was the strongest one in the family; he never complained of aches and illnesses, not even a headache.

By then, the realization sank in. This was really happening. Thankfully, it was the United States of America; everything had a cure, even cancer. I was so glad I was working at Ochsner Hospital. Ochsner health is one of the world's best and has been delivering expert care at its 46 various satellite hospitals with more than 370 health and urgent care centers. I worked at the main hospital. Ochsner's workforce includes more than 38,000 dedicated team members and over 4,700 employed and affiliated physicians. The physicians there were amazing, and the wealth of information available in the hospital library was tremendous. I began to read up on liver cirrhosis. We found that Ochsner had treatment and a rehabilitation program for those with liver cirrhosis. Andy could join this program, provided he never drank again. While I was sad, I was happy that at least now, we had diagnosed his illness. There was this amazing thing about Andy: no matter how much he drank, he always rose early the next morning and went to work. I had seen him work extremely hard even in India, and it was no different in the USA.

I told him, 'Listen, Andy. Even if you won't stop, at least ease up on the drinking. You have to allow your liver to heal. Drink only on the weekends.' But an alcoholic will never admit that they are an alcoholic. They would say, 'It's okay, not a big deal. I just need to relax and rest.' It's a pity. Had

Andy eased up on his drinking and joined Alcoholics Anonymous, the illness would not have consumed him. But he refused to admit that he had a drinking problem.

Andy refused to commit to the 'do not drink' rule. He refused to join Ochsner's rehabilitation program, too. And for as long as he continued drinking, he was not eligible to be listed on the liver transplant list. The doctors gave him medicines and repeated their admonition that he should refrain from drinking.

Andy took the medicines but not the admonition. The man who never took even an aspirin for pain was now having to take medicines for cirrhosis and pain. In spite of his illness, he somehow managed to keep working for a while; he kept a cheerful heart.

And then the vomiting began; he began to vomit blood on a few occasions. I was beside myself with worry and fear. But that didn't stop him from drinking. I did not understand this! I had known several people who drank daily and yet lived well into their eighties. Why couldn't that happen with Andy? That was my emotional mind speaking; my rational mind knew better. Being a positive thinker, I hoped Andy could beat this. In the medical sense, I knew that he could not recover unless he immediately stopped drinking and committed to the treatment plan wholeheartedly. I was extremely depressed; the habit he had acquired when he was a teen had totally ensnared him. It had him in a stranglehold, choking him slowly but surely.

Medically speaking, Stage 1 of cirrhosis of the liver generally exhibits no major complications. However, the swelling in Andy's legs and the development of esophageal varices were cause for worry. His illness was at an advanced stage. He developed portal hypertension and had to be given other medication. The lesions and the swelling on his legs became prominent. He would rest on weekends and sometimes sit in the sun, thinking the lesions would go away. I told him, 'Andy, the sun might help dry the skin lesions on his legs but would not cure him. You need to completely stop drinking. Can you do that?' but to no avail. Ironically, he started drinking even more, his excuse being that he was in pain!

That period of our lives was exhausting — our frequent visits to the hospital, the tension at home because of Andy's continued drinking, his refusal to wake up to reality, and my constant worrying. I had to attend to my children too and help them with their studies.

The doctors gave Andy abdominal taps, which were amazing; the distention in his abdomen would reduce, and his overall condition would improve. Andy was thrilled with this outcome. 'This is good! Because, even if I drink, they will remove all the fluid in my stomach, and I will be fine again,' he said. I was furious, frustrated, and helpless.

Somehow, life went on. We took it one day at a time and went with the flow. Our immigration woes continued, and the prospects of getting a green card looked bleak. It really didn't seem to matter anymore.

Every two months, Andy would vomit blood and require an abdominal tap. This was the new 'abnormally normal' routine for us. By then, the nurses in the ICU knew Andy well. He was not a good patient; he was reckless and fearless for the wrong reasons, and this was not appreciated. He wanted to continue smoking in the hospital, though he knew he could not drink there.

One evening, I received a phone call from a nurse in the ICU. She told me Andy had disappeared from his bed! They had looked everywhere in the hospital but could not find him. Her voice gave away her panic. I rushed to the hospital. And there, sitting on one of the benches near the entrance to the hospital and puffing away gaily on his cigarette, was good old Andy. Unbelievable! he had come down carrying the pole attached to the intravenous drip being administered to him! *What the heck*! I started shouting at him, oblivious to the passersby who were gawking at us. Andy finally came back to his bed, after finishing his smoke.

He never kept his appointments with the doctors. He never wanted to see a doctor unless there was an emergency. Sometimes, I felt he was indulging me by going to meet the doctors and getting admitted to the hospital.

In June 2002, Andy had another episode and started vomiting blood. This time, he stayed in the hospital longer. He was discharged on June 16. It was a huge scare; he had vomited far more blood than before. One of the doctors at the hospital told him, 'Andy, you have been playing with your critical condition for a long time. You really need to stop drinking *immediately*!' Andy replied, 'Doctor, it's okay. When one has to die, they will die. Perhaps I will die soon, and you too will join me later.' The shocked doctor left without saying another word.

When Andy came back home from that stay in the hospital, I told him, 'Andy, today is Father's Day. You are in a critical condition. The kids are little; they need their father. Can you take this seriously, at least now, and join the rehabilitation program so you can get on the transplant list? Unless you complete the rehab program, you will not be eligible for a transplant. The United States has amazing programs, and you will be okay.' He laughed it off and even went a step further to say, 'Well, if I die, you can remarry.' I was taken aback. He had never said anything like that before. 'Yes,' I retorted, 'as if one marriage is not enough.'

He seemed to have lost his ability to make a rational decision. The hour after he was discharged from the hospital, he bought himself a drink. His excuse was that it was Father's Day, and he had miraculously come back from the hospital in spite of vomiting excessive blood. It was impossible to talk sense into him. The next few months passed by without an episode of vomiting. He kept taking the abdominal taps and medicines on time but refused to stop his habitual drinking.

We tried to end that year on as positive a note as possible. The court case was behind us, and Andy's anti-battering program was over. Our I-485 step for immigration went through like a breeze. I was stressed, thinking Andy would not pass his medical examination for the I-485, but the results surprised me. That's probably because the authorities were mainly checking for communicable diseases, and none of us had any. We would now get our green cards in just a matter of months! How exciting! Maybe we would get our green cards, and Andy would go to India to visit and come back.

December 2002 stays crystal clear in my mind. I insisted that we dress up, take our official New Year photo, and send it to our friends and family. On the day we were to take this photo, Andy wasn't feeling well. He refused to dress up. It took me almost 5 hours to get him to wear a full suit. He said he would wear just the suit jacket and a shirt, with shorts to go with them! Shorts! He said the photo was to be taken only up to the waist, so why bother with trousers? I thought this was hilarious. Little did I realize that it would be our last annual family picture.

An End

January 19 came along soon. It was my birthday. Back in India, Andy celebrated my birthday every year, as usual, drinking with his friends. This invariably led to a fight and tears, and I would be spent by nightfall. My birthday in 2003 was pleasantly memorable. That was the only year in my entire married life that I did not cry on my birthday.

The birthday started on a good note, with cake and the works. I whipped up a great meal, and the four of us ate it with gusto. Andy began to drink, but thankfully, there were no fights or tears. I asked him, 'What happened? Is everything okay? He replied, 'What do you mean?'

'Well, it's almost midnight, but you haven't gotten into a fight with me. No shouting or beating?'

He looked surprised. I continued, 'Did you realize this is the first birthday that you did not fight with me, and I did not cry?' He smiled but did not say anything. We watched TV and retired for the night.

Andy's old friend from India, who now lived in Chicago, said he would be visiting us over the last weekend of January. Andy was excited; he hadn't met his friends from India ever since he arrived in the USA. This person had been his neighbor and childhood friend in Hyderabad. He said he would take a few days off to visit Andy. Andy kept talking about his friend at the gas station and at home 24/7.

His friend arrived that weekend. It was a fun time for Andy and us. We toured the French Quarter and cruised all over town. When we were home, Andy drank with his friend and drank excessively, even amid my protests. It reminded me of the times in Hyderabad when his friends would visit our home to binge drink with Andy, and I had to supply them with food continuously. This repeated itself over the next four days. I was very agitated and frustrated but relieved when his friend left.

That night, Andy said he wasn't feeling too well, but he was alert and wakeful. He also wanted me to pray with him, which was rather surprising. He fell asleep at 3 am after spending a rather restless night, after which I, too, was able to sleep.

I woke up late on Feb 3rd and had a delayed start. All of us were quite exhausted from the weekend of cooking, cleaning, and sightseeing when Andy's friend visited us. Andy said he did not have cigarettes and asked me to get him some on my way back home after dropping my daughter off at school. Upset, I said, 'You drank and smoked the entire four days. Take it easy and rest today. Don't smoke.' I left for work later that morning without buying him the cigarettes. He called me at work twice and reminded me about them. Agitated, I told him I would be coming home for lunch at around 12.30 pm and would bring them then. He said alright, adding that he was very tired and would probably take the day off from work. I agreed.

At around 12.25 pm, as I was getting ready to go home, I got a call from him again. 'Come home, Sharon. I am vomiting blood. It's not stopping. It's all over the place!' Andy could barely speak. My heart stopped. I immediately grabbed my bag and started running home, which was within walking distance of my workplace. That less-than-one-mile run was the longest of my life. My heart was pounding as I ran; I had a sense of foreboding.

The doctors had already told us that if Andy didn't stop drinking immediately, the varices would rupture soon. With a thousand thoughts racing through my mind, I opened the door to home, rushed in, and started calling out, 'Andy! Andy!' There was blood everywhere — on the bed, on the carpet, on the wall, all over the bathroom, on the floor. I found him vomiting; he was on the verge of fainting. I brought him out of the bathroom and made him sit on the sofa; he did not stop vomiting. I wiped the blood from his mouth, but more of it kept gushing out. It was unbelievable, like a movie. Everything seemed to be happening in slow motion.

I picked up the phone and called 911. I quickly told the operator the situation and asked her to rush an ambulance to my home. I ran to my neighbor and informed him. He came rushing, and together, we tried to revive Andy. I could not wait for the ambulance since it might take another ten minutes to arrive. I asked my neighbor, 'Will you help me get him into the car? I will then drive him to the hospital myself,' The neighbor, a big, burly man, carried Andy downstairs and placed him in the car's back seat. Thank God, the hospital was less than a mile away. As the neighbor was carrying him down the stairs, Andy tried to say something. I asked him not to talk, but he pulled my hand and said, 'Look after the children; I won't be back.'

Angry at him, I said, 'Don't say such things!' and began to cry. I took him to Ochsner Hospital. Even in the car, his vomiting and the horrible sound of his gurgling blood would not stop. It was awful to see him this way. I stopped in front of the Emergency entrance at the hospital and rushed in. I did not have sufficient money, so I let the docs know that I would be paying later. I showed them my employee ID card from Ochsner. They immediately brought a stretcher and took Andy in, after which I parked the car and went inside.

A team of doctors began to work on him. They did not allow me into the room. I was relieved that I had been able to bring him to the Emergency ward, where the doctors knew him and knew what to do. So much for the 911 call for an ambulance! Later, they sent me a bill – imagine that! I was grateful that our kids were at school and did not know what had happened. The memories of that day stayed with me for years; I could not get that awful and terrible sight out of my head.

Going back to work that day was out of the question, though my office was in the next building in the same hospital. I informed my manager about Andy's condition and said I could not come to work that day and the next day, too.

The doctors attending to Andy told me, 'Your husband's condition is critical. We can't predict what will happen in the next 24 hours.'

I said, 'Oh well, it's the same vomiting. He will be fine; he always pulls through.'

The doctor said, 'You don't understand. This time, he may not pull through.'

'When will he wake up? He seems unconscious. Or is he sleeping or sedated?'

'You're still not understanding me. His condition is critical. You seem to be taking it lightly.'

I looked at the doctor as if he was mad. I thought, they always say he's serious, but Andy comes through. Though I was working in the clinical research space in one of the top hospitals in the country, my mind could not wrap itself around the facts regarding Andy's condition. The medical professional in me could read the writing on the wall, but the spouse in me was optimistic. I had always thought of Andy as a fearless, unbeatable warrior in spite of his weaknesses. Nothing could keep him down.

When the kids came home that day, I took 75 dollars from my daughter. She was working weekends at a restaurant and had received her paycheck two days ago. Until then, I had been running around with exactly one dollar in my wallet. Neither Andy nor I had received our biweekly paycheck. I paid the co-payment of 75 dollars at the hospital, taking the money from my daughter. This left me with one dollar in my pocket again. I was grateful that I had medical insurance coverage from Ochsner.

All of Feb 4, Andy did not wake up. I kept badgering the doctors with the same questions, 'When will he be up? Why is he not waking up? Seeing him hooked to the IV tubes was nothing new, but in a strange way, it seemed to be different this time. Andy seemed to be sleeping yet not sleeping. I nudged him and tried to wake him up, saying, 'Andy, wake up, wake up! You're going to be okay. You've got to fight this! Why aren't you waking up? We should go home soon. You always come back home in a few days.' Amazingly, he opened his eyes a wee bit. Dazed, he nodded his head as if he understood what I was saying and mumbled something incoherent. He then drifted back to unconsciousness.

The nurse had removed Andy's thin gold chain and his two gold rings, one being his wedding band. She put this in a small box, which she handed me. The doctors asked me to bring the kids to see him. A sense of panic and foreboding of disaster filled me. When I tried to wake Andy up again, he gave me the same dazed look. I don't know if he noticed the children. I asked the doctors if he was in great pain. They said they didn't think so. They were pumping blood and plasma into his system. It looked as if he wasn't getting any better. His IV needles seemed to be bleeding, too. I did not understand any of this.

Seeing his father that way broke my little son. He cried a lot and wrote on the little box that had Andy's gold chain and rings, 'Daddy, I love you, come back.' I still have this little box with my son's handwriting on it. I took the kids back home; they seemed distracted. After serving them dinner, I returned to the hospital. I stayed with Andy, hoping he would say something. It was late at night when I got back home to the kids. It was such a relief that the hospital was less than a mile from home.

The next day, I woke up early to get the kids ready and send them to school before going to the hospital. I was getting ready to leave at around 7.30 am when I got a call from the hospital. They asked me to come immediately. I rushed there, telling the kids that the hospital called me, so I had to go.

My son went to school by bus, whereas I used to drop my daughter off by car daily. That day, I told her to walk to school. When I reached the hospital, the doctors said it was now just a matter of time. My mind could not grasp what they were saying. I kept hoping Andy would wake up. I gently nudged him again and said, "Andy, wake up. I am here! Why aren't you waking up?'

I could not process the fact that this was happening to me. He was really passing into his eternal rest. His eyes were closed, and his breathing was shallow. The doctor said I could leave and stand outside the door; I need not watch this happen. Andy was bleeding from the IV's that had been inserted into his body; It was awful! Blood was slowly trickling out of his mouth. His eyes were closed. This was like the climax of a movie in slow motion. I felt I was someone else. The doctor left the room. He was the same person to whom Andy had insouciantly said that he would die, and who knows, the doctor might follow him soon.

I stayed beside Andy, holding his hand and trying to wake him up. The nurse asked me if she needed to stay, but I seemed not to hear her. I kept watching Andy. With a boyish look on his face, he seemed so peaceful. I asked the nurse, 'Is he in pain?' She said, 'No. He's been sedated.' I thought I had seen a fleeting glimpse of the young man I had fallen in love with years ago. Time and age seemed to melt away. I felt one with him at that time, and strangely, as I felt so, his eyes seemed to light up for a minute. Or did I imagine it?

In that fleeting moment, I could see myself as one among the audience in a cinema hall, watching my entire life with Andy pass by.

The monitor was slowly flatlining. They tried to resuscitate him but to no avail. The monitor eventually flatlined, and he passed peacefully into heavenly glory. The nurse asked me to leave the room and began disconnecting the IVs from Andy. The doctor declared the time of death as 8.30 am. It was February 5, 2003. My life changed forever.

I never thought Andy would leave me. I have known several people who were alcoholics and yet lived to a happy 80. Nothing drastic ever happened to them! Never for a moment had I had thoughts of Andy's death.

I was in shock and pain. For a long time, I did not understand the enormity of what had happened.

They asked me if I had family around and told me to make arrangements for Andy's body to be taken to the funeral home. I told them that I had no money and no family around and did not know what was to be done. I wasn't prepared for this tragedy and the things that were to follow. With the one dollar I had and no family member or friend with me, I sat down on the steps of the hospital and wept bitterly. The hospital staff said they could transfer his body to the mortuary but could not keep him there for a long time.

I informed my manager. My colleagues were aghast since I had not told anyone that my husband was sick. They were wonderful people who said they would help. I called my parents and informed them, too. The chaplain of the hospital came and counseled me. I was numb and in shock that Andy was no more. I did not know who to ask for financial help. Apart from the dollar in my bag, I had a credit card with a balance of 50 dollars. Some people from Employee Services and International Relations at the hospital told me that I could go to the Social Security office and ask for financial help with the funeral arrangements. They directed me to a particular funeral home to make arrangements. I went to the funeral home and met with the funeral director, who was very kind. I remember that her name was Kim. She said they definitely needed a down payment for them to transport the body from the hospital mortuary to the funeral home.

My manager at the hospital, who was a doctor, came to know that I did not have any money. He and other doctors took up a collection drive among the hospital staff. I am eternally grateful for what my colleagues did for me.

I and the kids went to several churches nearby to see if a pastor would conduct the funeral service. I went to 12 different churches, but no pastor agreed to come — since we were not members of their churches! This was another nightmare. It was all very confusing as to what I needed to do since I never attended church back in India after I got married; I mostly accompanied my in-laws to the temple on a few occasions. My prayers were at home anyway. Andy wasn't religious and never believed in organized religion and its practices.

When we came to America, we sometimes went to church because of my son. I did not have a social life to call for help from any friend as well. My kids did go to a church with their friends and this continued religiously every Sunday. Andy never stopped them at any time. I called my parents for advice. They said this happens globally and in India too; if one is not a member of the church and does not pay tithe, then the church will not conduct the funeral service; one could rent a Pastor, though! in the United States. Unbelievable but true, and this was the case for marriage as well! The money on my credit card was almost gone since I had to spend money on gas for all the running around that was taking place.

That night, I went home and looked around to see if we had anything of value that I could sell. All we had was old stuff from the thrift stores. I knelt down with the kids and prayed to God to help us — to send us financial help.

Our two-bedroom home was a sight to behold, and I was oblivious. The kids were distraught and could not sleep. I sent them to the neighbor's home and tried to clean up the blood splattered on the walls, bathroom, carpet, and kitchen. There was blood on the walkway, too. I must have been exhausted by the grief and felt overwhelmed. I dozed off for a few hours and woke up in the morning to go back to the hospital. My colleague said she would be coming home that day to give me the money that was collected by the department.

Later that day, she came home, gave me the money, and spent some time with me. She was shocked that I was alone in the house, with blood all over the apartment. She asked me about my kids. I said they were with the neighbor but would be coming home soon.

I received a call from the hospital's Human Resources department saying that they had released money on compassionate grounds. A miracle! Indeed, the Hand of the Almighty was upon me again. With this money, I was able to finance the entire funeral and some money was left.

I was able to have Andy's body shifted from the hospital to the funeral home.

The staff member at the funeral home told me, 'Your husband will be bathed and clothed and presented for the funeral service.' I asked her, 'I need to get him his favorite clothes. Also, two of his friends and my aunt will be attending the funeral. We can hold the service on Feb 11 because that is a weekend.' She said, 'Yes, of course.'

With a heavy heart, the kids and I shopped for new clothes for Andy. It was terrible. I felt like a zombie in a movie. The kids looked at me strangely. Perhaps they could not understand the great sorrow I was going through. I bought Andy shoes, a black suit, a red shirt, which was his favorite color, and a tie. I made it a point to get a black-and-red tie, thinking it had to stand out. If it was just red, it would not stand out with the shirt. We drove back to the funeral home and handed over his new clothes.

After a few days, the kids refused to sleep in our neighbor's home. They wanted to come back home. Our nights were full of pain. I slept on the same bed I had shared with Andy. I had done my best to wash away the blood, but there were stains in places. The grief I felt was too great, and I was past thinking about the state of the apartment.

My aunt from DC and two of Andy's friends from Chicago arrived for the funeral service. Some of my colleagues and friends also attended. I still had not found a pastor to conduct the service. One of my colleagues told me to request the chaplain at Ochsner Hospital, where I worked, to conduct the same. It would not be a long one, perhaps 20 minutes or so. I requested the chaplain from the hospital to conduct the service and offered to pay him whatever little I could. He understood my predicament but was hesitant since a chaplain generally does not conduct a funeral service. Still, he was compassionate. He said he would visit my home and pray with the kids and me. Shocked at the condition of my home, he said he would not take any money but would be doing this for free. I thanked him profusely.

February 11. We had the funeral service. Surprisingly, a large number of people attended. The kids and I went early to the funeral home, where the prayer service was to be conducted. Kim took us to the place where Andy was resting. It was amazing — it looked as if the years and pain had left his body. There was no swelling on his face; he looked like a young man. I touched him and thought, He looks great, and yet he's so cold! The funeral services in the United States are indeed wonderful; they make the person look so alive! I touched his cheeks again and again as if to make myself believe that he was indeed gone. I thought he would sit up and say, as he always did, 'Don't worry, I am here. Nothing will happen.' It all seemed like a dream.

The service was done, and we returned home. Later, my aunt and Andy's friends from Chicago left. There was an outpouring of love and generosity from our neighborhood. For the next fortnight, I did not have to cook since several people bought us food. I went back to work in five days and sent the kids off to school in another five days. We had to go on, bringing a semblance of normality back into our lives. The best thing to do was to plunge back into work and school. The first few evenings after the service, I tried to rid our house of the remaining blood stains. The kind manager at our apartment complex asked to move into another apartment on the floor above at no additional cost. The love and warmth of strangers, who simply waved and said hello to us, was indeed overwhelming. The three of us tried to gather comfort from that.

And so, the show went on.

Strange Happenings

My family from India could not visit me in the aftermath of Andy's death. Going about all the death-related formalities all alone was strange and unsettling. My aunt, who did come for the funeral service, left the next day. I was alone with the kids, with no other extended family. I had decided to cremate Andy instead of having a regular burial. Cremation was cheaper since I did not have money for a burial; it was also the religious custom in Hinduism.

Two days after the cremation, the funeral home called me and asked me to take Andy's ashes. I was puzzled. I told Kim, the funeral director, 'I thought everything had been done. I don't know what to do with the ashes.' I was facing this situation for the first time in my life — being the protagonist at a funeral, doing everything on my own while managing two little kids. Every funeral I had attended in India had been a burial. I went with the kids to collect Andy's ashes. I asked Kim, 'What is the custom here? In India, it is a common Hindu custom that the eldest son immerses the ashes in the Ganga or a sacred river. But I have never seen it, let alone do it. I have only heard about this from friends and seen it in the movies.' Kim said, 'Very interesting! Here in the United States, we take the ashes around to the person's favorite places or place and scatter them there. Sometimes, if the departed one has left specific instructions on what is to be done with the ashes, we follow those instructions. People immerse the ashes in a river or scatter them in the mountains. Some people keep them at home.'

Hmm, I thought. I told Kim that I wanted to ask my husband's mother if I should send the ashes to her in India. Wistfully, I added, 'If only I could have afforded a proper burial for Andy.' Kim said with a kindly look, 'Don't worry. You really did your best. He looked handsome. I am sure he must be smiling from heaven.'

I hadn't known that I had to bring my own urn to take the ashes in, so Kim put these into a box at the funeral home and put the ashes into it. I wasn't sure if I was ready for this. The kids looked rather shaken. Anyway, I took the box and held it close to my chest for a little while. We prayed for a minute and placed the box in the front passenger seat of our car. It was rather shocking to see how a human is reduced to ashes. It is rightly said: 'For dust you are, and to dust you will return.'

After arriving at our home, I opened the box. The ashes were completely white. I was seeing the ashes of a human being for the first time in my life. The kids went out to play with their friends. I carefully placed the urn on the mantelpiece. That night, I called Andy's mother, who lived in Hyderabad, to ask her if I should send the ashes to India. His mom wailed and screamed on the phone, 'You can do whatever you want with them! I don't want them back in India; you have killed my son. Even if you send them and the money, my son is gone!' Those were her exact words. I suppose everyone has their own way of grieving. The loss of a son is terrible for any mother, and so it was for my mother-in-law. What made it sadder was that she had lost her second son a few years ago.

Over the next day or two, I watched a few YouTube videos to learn more about the immersion of ashes. I was keen to do whatever I could for Andy.

That Saturday, I told the kids that we, as a family, would do whatever we could to honor Andy's memory. I said, 'We will drive him to all his favorite places, like the Exxon gas station he worked at, Harrah's Casino, Treasure Chest, Popeyes, the causeway bridge over Lake Pontchartrain, St. Charles Street, and so on.' Pausing briefly, I added, 'I don't think we can enter the Claiborne Projects. That's a dangerous place.'

I told my son, 'We have to come back home, close to the Mississippi River, and you, being the only son, should immerse the ashes.'

Poor kid. He looked up at me innocently and said, 'Okay, ma.' We prayed for a bit. I carried the urn back to the car, and we drove around to the places I had mentioned. As I drove, I talked to Andy and recollected our trips to these places as if he were right there, sitting next to me. At each place, we stopped for a few minutes. The kids didn't say much; I think it was rather traumatizing for them. Most of the time, they stayed silent.

Soon, we found ourselves on the mighty Clairborne Road, as Andy called it, "the mighty Claiborne." I realized with consternation that we were approaching the Projects. I told the kids, 'Well, here come the Projects. Your dad had many friends here. He hung out at the car repair shop here. I've come here with him just once.' The projects were notorious for the high rate of violent crimes. In fact, it was known to be one of the most violent housing projects in the United States. Since Andy had worked in a gas station close to this place, he had friends living there. He spent time with them, often hanging out with the street hoodlums. I was nervous about entering the area, especially with the kids.

Within a minute of my saying this to the kids, the car began to wobble. We had a flat tire! I stopped the car to take a look.

Both the front tires had a flat. This happened exactly at a traffic light leading into the Projects. Of all the places! Stunned, I and the kids were completely taken aback. A passerby hailed us and said, 'Hey! Aren't you Andy's wife? What happened?' It looked like he was one of Andy's friends. He'd probably seen me when I picked Andy up from the Exxon gas station where he used to work.

Holding my breath, I said in a composed voice, 'Yes, I am Andy's wife. He's not with me. I have a flat.' The man checked the front tires and said, 'Boy, both tires! Strange. Drive slowly into the lane. I can tell you where to go to get these fixed.' I got into the car and slowly drove it towards the mechanic shop he guided me to. Somehow, we got there in a couple of minutes, the car dangerously wobbling. I told the kids, "Keep calm, ok? Don't get out. And don't say anything about Daddy.'

I do not understand at this point in time why I said this since he was well loved there. Or maybe I was afraid and did not want to draw too much attention! Not sure of my state of mind at that point in time. One thing I knew was that I was definitely afraid of entering the projects, known for their crime and violence.

A mechanic at the garage fixed the tires. Before we got out of the car, I took the urn that held Andy's ashes and hurriedly placed it in the trunk. I threw a jacket over the box to conceal it. As the mechanic was working on the tires, I realized that the three of us stuck out in the neighborhood. Though I tried to appear calm, I felt extremely tense.

After an hour that seemed like a million years, the tires were fixed. I paid him the money and thanked him. The mechanic and a couple of other guys at the garage waved goodbye to us. One of them said to me, 'Hey, say hello to Andy from us and tell him we will see him one of these days.' I smiled, nodded, and we left.

Though a little shaken, we felt lucky we were to have run into people who had hung out with Andy! I go back in time to that moment and think of what I felt. In spite of having my husband's ashes right beside me and being full of grief and pain, I held my composure.

We stopped at Popeyes. Opening the trunk, I placed the box in the front passenger seat again. I was happy we had 'taken Andy' to all of his favorite places. A little later, we went to the mighty Mississippi, where my son had to immerse his father's ashes. Standing by the river brought up a fresh wave of emotions. We often hung out as a family here, jogging, walking, and taking pictures. Andy had sometimes flown kites here with the kids as I lazed around watching them.

We climbed down the riverbank. I told my son he had to hold the urn. My son back then was a thin, wiry little child in his 3rd grade. He could not hold the urn. I told him, 'Sam, I cannot immerse the ashes. You have to.' He replied woefully, 'Ma, the urn is very heavy!' 'Okay then, let me hold it with you. And then you can tilt the urn so the ashes fall into the water,' I said.

Then I added, 'Oh wait! The water is still. There are no waves at all. This is strange! Most of the time, the boats and ships sailing by send ripples of water to the banks. If we immerse the ashes now, they might fall onto the rocks, and people might stamp on them. That would be disrespectful. Let's wait until a wave comes in to take his ashes into the river.' And there we were, my son and I holding the urn of ashes and my daughter standing beside us, watching.

We waited, but nothing happened. I said, 'I don't know what to do now. I wish a few mighty waves came and swept the ashes into the middle of the river.' And lo! Out of nowhere, as if the Almighty was answering my prayer, the water began to ripple, and huge waves came by. I was excited and said to my son, 'Tilt the urn, tilt the urn! Pour the ashes into the water.' We tipped the ashes out. And in less than a minute, Andy's ashes were gone, taken away by the mighty Mississippi. My son began to tremble and cry out, 'Daddy, Daddy!' and fell down on the banks of the river. He was badly shaken but unhurt. My daughter was stunned. She ran up the bund and stood several feet away from us. She refused to come down to where we were standing. My son and I climbed back up onto the bund slowly.

Immersing the ashes had been an overwhelming moment for all of us. Shaken, the three of us went back home and showered. None of us felt like eating. We sat there until late into the night, lost in our thoughts. I pondered over the strange happenings in the past few days.

The pain and grief stayed with us for weeks after that, though the children were somewhat quicker to get back to normalcy. I did not understand how to heal. People at work were very helpful; they said they empathized with me. Phone calls poured in from all over the world. Friends and family said 'they understood.' But I wondered if they really did. How could they understand the searing pain cutting through my bones every moment of every day? I never wore my heart on my sleeve at any time in my life and still do not, people thought I was okay.

As the years rolled by, I realized that the pain does reduce a bit but never goes away. It simply becomes a part of you; it is always there. Charlie Chaplain was right when he said, 'To truly laugh, you must be able to take your pain and play with it.'

I think I have learned to do this since, often, no one else knows the pain I undergo on a daily basis.

My Parents in the USA

I did not have time to immerse myself in grief after the death of my beloved Andy. Grief is a process; one must take time to heal, rest, recharge, and move on in life. To be the strongest version of themselves for themselves, their children and their other loved ones. Grief makes you do irrational things that often go against what you would have done under normal circumstances.

From the day Andy passed away, every time I called up my parents, they would say, 'Let us come to the United States. We can come and stay with you. You do not need to show the usual minimum bank balance; the visa will be granted on compassionate grounds due to the death of your spouse.' This conversation took place on a daily basis, every time I called them. I felt weary and pressurized. I do not think they understood the grief I felt; it was their need to move to the US as usual. The agony of losing Andy was already too much to handle. If I brought my parents over, I would be adding severe financial stress to my grief. Their tickets and their expenses in the USA would be a burden to me. My earlier experience with Dad in the USA was still fresh in my mind. I had limited money.

My experiences in America made me a lot wiser. I was very different from the girl my parents knew in India. Circumstances have changed me a lot in recent years.

I reluctantly sent them the documents for their visa through FedEx since they cost nothing to me to work on their visa sponsorship documents. I regretted that decision almost immediately and wished I could take the documents back, but what was done was done. I hoped my parents would, for some reason, not get the visa. But they did.

I did not want to bring them to the United States. My plan was to build a home for them in India. I had been paying their medical expenses ever since I started earning a decent amount in the United States. All of my mom's retirement money had been spent. Ever since my mom retired, it was difficult for them to manage the home. As for Dad, his jobs were erratic. He stopped working after Mom had a heart attack in October 1997.

As for my brother and his wife, they never worked for several years. It was after Mom retired that they started working, and even then, only intermittently. Both of them had meager salaries, and their son had a chronic medical problem that required constant medical care. They were a burden on my parents. And my parents themselves were dependent on me. It was a vicious cycle.

From 1999, when I got the job at Ochsner Hospital, to 2016, when Dad passed away, I sent money to my parents and brother every month. After Mom and Dad passed away, I continued to support my brother, his wife, and his son until all of them passed away, one by one, each under tragic circumstances that left me in deep anguish. I must admit that it was very difficult to shoulder their expenses even as I was building my career and taking care of my children in the States. I did have moments of angst, wishing that my brother and his wife changed their attitude towards life and work and started fending for themselves. I had several moments of angst during those years. Still, I considered it my duty to support my family and did so.

Thankfully, my brother was very appreciative of what I did for him and his family. He and I had drifted apart in our teens and stayed that way for 20 years or so. We came together again under extremely tragic circumstances when our dad passed away.

In retrospect, I do not think my parents considered me a young widow who was almost overwhelmed by life. I think they could not understand me. They thought that I was stronger than I really was. I realized this only after they came to live with me in the States.

I realized I had evolved into someone very different from them in some fundamental ways, though I retained some of their traits. I felt almost guilty to have come to the United States and was apologetic. It had been my parents' dream since the time I was five years old that they would emigrate to the United States. Perhaps they did not think of the toll it would take on my health, finances, and my children. Or perhaps they thought the loss of a violent husband was a relief for me. From their perspective, I think they were right. Many of my friends, too, thought it was better that Andy had passed away, but I had never felt that way. I wanted him to stop drinking and lead a normal life as a happy father. But who knows, maybe I was not normal for wishing for a 'happily ever after,' knowing the kind of person Andy was.

Many Indian parents wish to live vicariously through their children, thrusting their dreams and ambitions onto them. The children feel guilty if they don't achieve these ambitions or if they don't share these ambitions in the first place. And by the time they realize it, it is too late. This is especially seen when one of the children is highly successful and another is not. Parents want all their children to be successful, but this seems rather unrealistic to me. When I was going through the motions, I did not realize it, but what was done had been done. I have no regrets.

On the other hand, I see children who leave their parents and cut them off completely after the parents have poured their life's savings into them. I am for helping parents, but then, one has to take care of oneself too, lest the vicious cycle should continue and you, as a parent, become a burden on *your* children. I was a child of circumstances. Sometimes, these circumstances led me from one hasty decision to another. Thankfully, though, I have the inherent trait of fighting and rising up. I have been doing that since I was a teenager.

In this aspect, the American culture should be appreciated. Americans expect their children to move out when they are 18 and start fending for themselves. Parents here do not expect anything much from their children. At the same time, there is a sad aspect too. All too often, parents here are left to die in old age homes, lonely and sad. It's a vicious cycle; at times, rather extreme behavior on the part of parents and children leads to repercussions that affect grandchildren.

In the words of Gibran, 'Your children are not your children. They are the sons and daughters of Life's longing for itself. They come through you but not from you, and though they are with you, yet they belong not to you.'

That balance of 'give and take' and expectations was not in order in my life. I have gone through a lot to come to where I am now. Though the view from my perch has often looked great, the pain I have endured and the sacrifices I have made have left me spent and mentally exhausted in the past. But I have grown stronger. The wounds have healed; only the scars remain.

Why is it that sometimes the child has to become the parent? But now all that is done. One can do nothing about the past but learn to be wiser and not make major decisions when in grief and pain. I regretted my big decision of agreeing to bring my parents to the USA after Andy's death. Both of them had health problems with no medical insurance. I couldn't begin to imagine what would happen if they fell sick in the USA. What do the flight attendants say to passengers? 'Put on your oxygen mask before helping someone else put their mask on.' I wish I had thought of this myself. It struck me only much later when one of my dear friends mentioned it.

Andy's death thus paved the way for my parents to get their visa to fly to the United States. I had to borrow money from a colleague to buy their tickets. I repaid this colleague later. My parents landed safely. They did bring their medications for at least six months. Hospitalization is a nightmare in the USA, so I hoped they'd never have to be admitted to a hospital here. The kids were overjoyed at seeing their grandparents, whereas I was under greater stress than ever. I became increasingly frustrated and missed Andy all the more.

Thinking it would be good if Dad worked somewhere during his stay in the States, I reached out to Andy's friends in Chicago. It was easier to find work there than in New Orleans.

One of Andy's friends asked Dad to go to Chicago. He said he would help him find a job in a hotel. Four of Andy's friends stayed together as roommates, so I told Dad, 'Why don't you go alone? Mom can remain here. It will be better that way.' Dad agreed and went to Chicago.

Mom was heavily dependent on Dad, who treated her like a princess and did everything for her. Bringing her breakfast, tea, lunch, dinner, and injections, laying out her clothes, and combing her hair — Dad did everything for her! I could not do all this. I was dealing with my own work, the kids, their activities, and the grief from Andy's loss. Also, my health took a turn for the worse. I began to suffer from acute attacks of hives, which left me exhausted physically and emotionally. Maybe my stress and grief aggravated the medical condition.

At times, I had to use the epi-pen, and I was on three types of antihistamines for several years until I moved to New York. Strange as it may seem, my mom could not understand why I was full of grief. But how could she? My parents had a normal marriage. I find it amazing when people with normal marriages say 'they understand.' I will never profess to be in the shoes of another person. Nor will I advise anyone else except my children on marriage.

Increasingly frustrated, I asked my mom to help me with the cooking and cleaning. Perhaps I came across as a little rough to her; I am not sure. My mom, a genteel lady, could not deal with my bluntness. I have never had the habit of mincing words. My mom and I had grown apart over the years, and I had been away from her for too long.

And then the inevitable, what I had dreaded happened. My mom fell sick. And there it was, the medical expenses. I had no choice but to take her to the hospital. The bills came thick and fast. I was extremely upset. My mom felt uncomfortable with me. She did not want to stay with me any longer. She didn't want to travel alone to Chicago, either. I had to pay for my dad to come and take her to Chicago.

For the rest of that year, my kids and I were in New Orleans, and my parents were in Chicago. Later, they moved to California. With their departure, I honestly felt a bit relieved. The children and I were back to our old normal selves and were able to manage, though I kept paying for some of my parents' expenses although they moved to Chicago. My dad sent his money to my brother and his family in India every month. I never asked my parents about the money I had spent on them. I was more than happy to be with my children, and we tried to heal.

My mom fell quite ill in Chicago. She was already a diabetic and a heart patient. I could no longer afford their medical expenses. She did not like the United States. She wanted to return to India. She missed my brother and, most of all, my brother's only son.

I was back to buying tickets again, this time for my mom's trip to India. The following year, my dad suffered from chest pain when he was in California and was admitted to the hospital. His manager called me at 8 am one day and said, 'Come immediately. Your father's condition is serious. You have to come and take him since I cannot take that responsibility.' I told him I couldn't come immediately. The final interview for a job I had applied for was scheduled that morning; too much was at stake. I said my son and I would fly out to California that night. My dad's manager and his colleagues thought I was being cruel. So did my mother and my relatives, who called me and scolded me. But I was clear-headed and angry, too; this was a bit much for me to handle. I knew what I was doing; I had to take this job for the sake of my children and our future. I attended the interview and got the job! That job has been the best in my entire career.

Had I taken that morning flight instead, it would have jeopardized my entire career and my kid's future.

I met my dad in California. He was in recovery. He wanted to go back to India that week itself. The doctors cleared him to fly. But since he was weak, someone would have to accompany him. I was at my wit's end since neither my son nor I would be able to accompany him just then. I was waiting for the new job.

After hurried consultations with my children, we decided that my daughter, who was working in New Orleans while also studying there, would come to California and accompany Dad to India. She did so, returning to the USA in a few days. She then had to make up for the classes she had missed at the university. I felt deeply agitated, considering my severely depleted finances, but I was happy that Dad had recovered and that he and Mom were comfortable at home in India. That is where they felt they truly belonged. I also felt better because it was easier to take care of my parents when they were in India, considering that I had to finance their trips up and down the country along with their medical expenses, piling up my credit card bills.

Dr. Sharon Joshua John

My Entire Family in India is Gone

I was exposed to death at a very young age and thought it was the greatest thing that could happen. The child who had asked her Nainamma, 'When are you going to die,' was long gone. The grief and pain the death of a family member causes have taken its toll. I am grateful for the time spent with my parents, my brother, his wife and son, though it was mostly over the phone, video calls, and letters in the past two decades. I do think I could not have got this sense of peace without my faith in God.

Death is inevitable; the day we are born, the Maker writes the day of our death, too. I have lost six members of my family — Andy, Dad, Mom, my brother, his wife, and his son — all of whom were dependent on me financially and emotionally. My brother and his family all left at rather young ages, within a span of two years, from 2020 to 2022. I have often felt exhausted, that I had to be the strong one for everyone all the time. I felt mentally drained, but my faith in God kept me going.

I do feel lonely at times, with no family left in India. The phone calls to them were a part of my everyday life. I anxiously waited for nightfall and morning so I would call up India. As my children grew up and got busy with their own lives, I would be on the phone to India for more than an hour on the weekends. That void will take some time to fill.

The financial burden of my parents' brother and his family's expenses continued from 1999 to 2022. I took care of their rent, groceries, medical bills, and the expenses related to their final trip from this world. At times, I was frustrated and angry that I could never save anything, no matter how hard

I worked or how much my salary increased. I battled with myself during these times — I was miserly with myself but gave others more than I could.

But then, I would think of my Nainamma's grief, telling myself that my situation was much better than hers had been. Few of her children were highly successful but they did not help her. Instead, they turned their backs upon her when she was sick and in dire need of their help. Though she was always ready and willing to leave this world, she was sad that these children of hers never called or visited her. I thought of what she would have done in my situation. I tried my best to help my family unconditionally. I lived by the day and continue to do so now. We don't lack for anything. At the end of the day, alone we come, and alone we go. The beggar and the king lie in the same 6 feet. Neither of them can take any treasure back in their death. I have come to a vantage point in my life where I feel much at peace about having done what I could do for my family. One must be able to live with oneself; that is all that matters.

The death of my brother was the greatest loss for me, mainly because we lost precious time with each other over the years and could never fully make up for that.

Like I said, we drifted apart during our teens and barely spoke to each other for a long time. The chasm of silence existed for several years. I tried to reach out to him but to no avail.

Our paths were divergent, except when it came to financial help, which I sent him through my parents. Fate, however, struck a terrible blow through the death of our father. After that, my brother reached out directly to me in 2016. I felt devasted at the great sorrows he had faced. The congenital illness of his son had progressed to an advanced stage. He lost his wife in 2020 and his son in June 2022. The tragedy of his son's passing took a toll on him, and he left this world, albeit peacefully, within two months of that event.

During the daily phone calls I had with my brother from late 2016 to 2022, I realized that we had lost our childhood rather early in life at my maternal grandmother's home.

Both of us cherished the time we spent in Maredpally with our Nainamma who was our paternal grandmother; our life there was simple and joyful. Though the circumstances had changed and decades had passed, we found ourselves being the little kids we used to be. Strangely, my brother reminded me of Dad, and we reconnected as if nothing had changed from when we had been ten years old! In spite of the pain, we laughed, thinking of our childhood pranks. I think my brother was the only one who was grateful for my moral and financial support during his dire times. When my journey in life is over, I trust I will see him and the others I have lost.

Once again, I ponder on the breath of life. What is a man without the breath of life? Adam was made of sand until God breathed the breath of life into his body, and he began to live. Dust we are, and to dust do we return. We can hold on to memories and think about the good times we have had. I ponder over the fact that, though I was in India in the early part of my life, I could not spend much meaningful time with my parents and brother. Now, they are together, united in death. Was it my destiny that had prepared me to lose all these family members through their untimely deaths?

When I look at old pictures, I feel wistful. I am also grateful and cherish the lovely moments I spent with them. For almost 24 years, I spoke to my family in India every day. I had great phone conversations. When people are in great suffering, and when they leave this world, we comfort ourselves that death is not the end but the beginning of a life beyond.

Finding my Emotional Feet Again

My children were very little when they came to the United States. My son was in the 2nd grade, and my daughter was in the 7th. They have always been loving children, their hearts filled with innocence and kindness. Over the years, they have grown up into fine human beings. They have survived a lot and achieved a lot through sheer determination and hard work. I strongly believed in leading by example, as my parents did for my brother and me.

From the 8th grade to the time she completed high school, my daughter studied at Riverdale Middle School. She was a star student, winning several awards at the school and district levels and representing the state of Louisiana at the INTEL Science and International Engineering Fair twice. She won at the Science fair on both occasions. She was in the local newspapers quite often and was an all-rounder, being good at academics, extra-curricular activities, and sports. She was invited to attend the presidential classroom, which was a great honor for a teenager of her age.

My son excelled in whatever he did. He was on the honor roll in his elementary school, Ella Dolhonde, in New Orleans and continued to do well in academics in the later years. He, too, attended the Presidential classroom. As a child, he was happy-go-lucky and made new friends easily in our apartment complex.

Andy's demise gave the three of us a lot of pain and grief. I remember Andy as his own person; he lived life large, on his own terms. I know he is in a better place. Though he didn't live long, he had a good life in India, and in the short span of five years he spent in the United States. Very few people can predict the time and hour of their own death. Andy was one of those privileged ones since his last words, as I was rushing him to the hospital, were, 'I won't come back; take care of the children.'

He never spoke in the hospital; he just lay there dying. Along with the good memories of my time with him, I have terrible memories of his drinking and his verbal and physical abuse. It took me a good ten years to heal from the physical pain I felt in my heart almost every day.

The month we lost him, I took the rash decision of bringing my parents to the United States, thinking they would bring me and my children some moral support. But I did not realize that they, though similar to me in some ways, were fundamentally very different from me.

They did not understand me. I was a young woman who had mostly grown up on my own since the age of 18. I think of Gibran's words again. 'Your children are not your children. They are the sons and daughters of Life's longing for itself. They come through you but not from you. And though they are with you, they belong not to you. You may give them your love but not your thoughts, for they have their own thoughts. You may house their bodies but not their souls. For their souls dwell in the house of tomorrow, which you cannot visit, not even in your dreams. You may strive to be like them but seek not to make them like you. For life goes not backward nor tarries with yesterday. You are the bows from which your children as living arrows are sent forth.'

I am happy that my kids were still very young when I went through the worst of my emotional and financial turmoil. They were focused on their studies, oblivious to the financial problems I faced in the two years after Andy's death. I was depressed but continued living; I have never worn my heart on my sleeve. I buried all the grief and pain in my heart, saying one has to do what one has to do. I was determined to make it to the top of my career ladder.

Those two years were crucial for my children. My daughter completed high school and joined the University of New Orleans. A few months later, I got a great job in New York. I moved with my son while my daughter continued to study at the university. Much to my displeasure, she dropped out of the university a few months later. She wanted to work and find her own path. I had no problem with her finding her own path as long as it included getting a solid educational foundation.

Education has always been a big thing for me. In fact, it was my education that helped me find myself and hold on to myself through the difficult years of my marriage. I tried my best to get my daughter to go to college, even in New York, but she did not budge from her decision to work instead. She chose to stay in New Orleans, after which she moved to North Carolina, where she now lives.

She completed her schooling, after a rather lengthy break of a decade or so, from one of the most reputed universities in the United States. She finally graduated from the University of North Carolina, USA. And for this, I am extremely proud of her. I told her she had accomplished more than most others; going back to studying after such a long break was a big achievement!

A large part of my life has been stressful. I did not have any time to stop and think for myself. I felt weary of being the strong one all the time — for myself, my children, and my family in India.

My son has grown up to be the fine young gentleman I wanted him to be. I relish his concern and feel rather privileged to be his mom. He has been instrumental in my finding my emotional feet again during the latter part of my life in the United States. His words of wisdom often confound me, and I sometimes exclaim that I wish he had been older when I was younger. This is rather funny, coming from a parent. He continues to influence me with his quiet strength and kindness even today. Until he completed his Bachelor's degree, he sometimes lived in the college dormitory or with roommates. But he always came home during the weekends and term-ending holidays.

During that time, I became much closer to him than before and learned a lot from him. I still do, and I often ask him for advice. I am grateful for his guidance and his gentle, respectful, yet firm way of showing me that it is okay to invest in myself. I am amazed at my son's resilience and fortitude. He had to grow up faster than his peers and coped well with the absence of a father when compared to his peers. When we lived in New Jersey, I was on the road, travelling on business every month. My son was underage then but managed quite well.

I would leave the refrigerator stocked. He never complained. Even now, he doesn't complain. He has taught me to be kind to myself and has been my anchor so far. This has been a long and arduous journey, and I am still learning how to do it. I am definitely much better now at forgiving myself, being kind to myself, and investing in myself than I was years ago.

I do not think I gave myself sufficient time to heal from the grief of losing Andy. I lost myself in my career and in taking care of my children, my parents, my brother, and his family.

I felt a huge responsibility towards all of them. Curiously, I almost felt guilty for being successful in my career.

It took me several years to understand that, as a parent and individual, I, too, have several faults. I have learnt not to be hard on myself.

Dr. Sharon Joshua John

Making a Career in the USA

My career is the highlight of my achievements. From a young age, I dared to dream big — very big! — for a girl in India those days. I have risen up the ranks, working my way up from being a lowly fee collector at a typewriting institute in India to becoming a successful, highly accomplished global executive and corporate leader. I am well-travelled, and continue to travel globally, something I could never have dreamt of 20-odd years ago.

I must say that my mother has been instrumental in educating me. And the love for reading, which she instilled in me, exposed me to a variety of situations, people, fields, and places all over the world. Early on, she exposed me to great literary works that inspired me. She was a woman of few words who led by example. Her love, though not expressive, was shown by her acts, and I cherish it.

The accolades and awards I have received, and the wonderful colleagues I have worked with have been instrumental in challenging me to be the best version of myself. I have lived and worked in Switzerland, a country my mom would have loved to visit. Sadly, she did not live to see that day. I have travelled, and continue to travel, to Europe and have seen a good part of that world, be it for business or for pleasure.

My parents loved to travel. I got the love for travel from them, mainly from my mother. My mom worked in the Central Government of India and had a perk called Leave Travel Concession, which allowed us to travel all over India every two years or so. Not many people had this privilege when I was a kid.

I grew up seeing my dad love his work. He always said, 'Companies are never loyal to you. *You* be loyal to your skills and love what you do, and you will shine.' My parents were not in the field of science, but they encouraged me to use my talents and flair and provided me with the best of everything when I was a child. They sent me to the best schools and the best colleges. When I got married, my life nosedived financially, and my education took a hit. Life was challenging, but this did not deter me. I picked my broken self up and persevered. I supported myself financially and emotionally and got my Master's degree and my doctorate.

My dad always boasted about my accolades to others. I did not understand my mom for a long time, but later, I understood her quiet love and endearing affection, as reflected in the wonderful letters and greeting cards she sent me without fail when I came to the United States. She kept up this habit until she passed away in 2008. Her letters were full of encouragement and filled with words of love and pride. I treasure them.

In her last letter to me, which she wrote in 2007, Mom wrote, *'May God bless you abundantly on this, your birthday, and grant you many more years with good health, peace, and happiness. It was a great blessing when you were born. We are blessed to be your mom and dad. May God renew your spirit and grant you new thoughts and ideas. May He give you new victories in all and everything you touch and undertake. You are a conqueror. Trust God completely in all that He does, though you may not understand right now. God is with you and will carry you on His wings.'* Such kind, uplifting words! As I write about Mom now, I realize that I did not understand her well. I wasn't too confident; I was this rough, gawky girl, while my mom was perfect and too beautiful for me. I, therefore, felt more comfortable with Dad than with her.

Mom used to tell me, 'A soft answer turneth away wrath.' At that time, I thought this was funny, but the wise words of my elders remained with me, and I passed them on to my children.

I have a challenging, stressful, yet exciting career in the field of clinical research. I find myself making a difference in people's lives. This is the most fulfilling and rewarding experience one can have.

Dr. Sharon Joshua John

The Hand of God

I cannot forget that the hand of the Almighty has always been upon me. I can't forget the perilous times during which He held my hand and walked with me. The times when I thought He had left, only to find that He had not; the times I was angry, but He was patient with me. When I tried to end my life, He was right there with me; on the days I felt alone, He was by my side.

My faith in God has held me together in spite of grief and loss. I have failed several times, and sometimes, haven't been the person I wanted to be. I have gathered strength from the Almighty and helped myself. I sometimes wonder how I have come this far. And then I realize it's because of His blessings.

I feel a deep sense of loss, thinking of the ones who are not with me anymore. At the same time, I feel great joy thinking of the ones who are. The poster child of her parents, the girl who was rebellious and suicidal, the girl who survived emotional and physical abuse and miscarriages, eventually turned resourceful and came out triumphant. Dare I say, 'A rose shall always be a rose?' The girl who was at peace initially journeyed through anger and pain and has finally returned to peace. Isn't this — to survive and thrive amidst misfortune — what makes us all human?

The journey has been painful yet beautiful. I credit this to the Almighty.

Looking Ahead

I have finally begun to take care of myself. I've been running the race for far too long. This is something I could have done earlier; I am committed to doing it, at least now. It's never too late to do a good thing.

I rest on hope that has bloomed again, inspired by the heroes who left a part of their spirit in me. The indomitable and resilient spirit of rising up from pain has been my forte and the mantra I inherited from my parents and my Nainamma. My hands are on the free armor and weapons they have left behind to be true to yourself and rest in the arms of the Almighty.

I have a lot to be thankful for. For instance, the many people who have had a significant impact on me. My children have been the rock of my life. They have brought me much joy and have been instrumental in my perseverance over the years.

The volatile Andy, who made me feel safe and special when he was not verbally or physically abusing me, was unwittingly responsible for making me strive for excellence.

I am truly grateful to my parents and my Nainamma, who have been instrumental in shaping my life. And to my brother. Though I had grown apart from him for several years, we became close once again in the last few years of his life. This had a surprising and refreshing effect on me. I have not forgotten the past; it has made me a better person. With several extraordinary experiences behind me, I look forward to the rest of my life in the company of the people I love.

I am eternally grateful to a few others who believed in me. Dr. Chary, my beloved guide and mentor during my PhD years. Her support was unwavering, even when it took longer than expected to complete the program. I am grateful to all the teachers from my formative years and my professors who encouraged me. Dr. Fingerman, who sponsored me to America as a post-doctoral research fellow, was responsible for my taking the big leap from the well that was Hyderabad to the ocean that is the USA. Dr. Money helped me by sponsoring my green card at Ochsner Hospital. I am indebted to several of my managers, who shaped my career and motivated me.

While writing this book, I met Ganesh Vancheeswaran. Ganesh has not only been the editor of this book but has also motivated me during another trying part of my life — from 2020 to 2022 when I lost my brother and his family. He has helped me focus on the book and, in general, the things in life that really matter. He has been a true friend and a mentor.

Writing this book has been draining and yet exhilarating. It has been a catharsis for me.

My journey has been perilous yet fulfilling, with all its ups and downs. Isn't that what life is all about? Though I didn't realize this or acknowledge it in the past, I think I have done incredibly well for myself. In spite of the turbulence in my life, I steeled myself to stay on the path to academic and professional growth. And indeed, to personal growth, too. I believe compassion for the less fortunate is the first tenet of the Almighty, and I have tried my best to be compassionate and discharge my responsibilities towards my loved ones.

Unfortunately, in living for the others, I forgot to live for myself. I am redressing this imbalance at this point in my life.

I find myself in a joyous place, celebrating the lives of the loved ones who have gone ahead and celebrating love with those who are with me. I look at my life in wonder; I have risen from humble beginnings to places of honor that the Almighty has been kind to bestow upon me.

www.ingramcontent.com/pod-product-compliance
Lightning Source LLC
Chambersburg PA
CBHW061346310726
48974CB00001B/223